P9-CRF-653

DREAMWORKS®

BEE MOVIE™

The Junior Novel

HarperCollins®, 🎬, and HarperEntertainment™
are trademarks of HarperCollins Publishers.

Bee Movie: The Junior Novel
Bee Movie™ & © 2007 DreamWorks Animation L.L.C.
Printed in the United States of America. All rights reserved.
No part of this book may be used or reproduced in any manner whatsoever without
written permission except in the case of brief quotations embodied in critical articles and reviews.
For information address HarperCollins Children's Books,
a division of HarperCollins Publishers,
1350 Avenue of the Americas, New York, NY 10019.
www.harpercollinschildrens.com

Library of Congress catalog card number: 2007929094
ISBN 978-0-06-125178-8

Book design by John Sazaklis
❖
First Edition

DREAMWORKS®

BEE MOVIE™

The Junior Novel

Adapted by
Susan Korman

HarperEntertainment
An Imprint of HarperCollinsPublishers

CHAPTER ONE

Barry B. Benson was a blur of black and yellow as the bee rushed around, getting ready for the biggest day of his life. Barry felt his antennae vibrate.

Brrrring! Brrrring!

He quickly finished brushing his teeth, then answered his phone. "Hello?"

"Barry!" a familiar voice greeted him. It was Adam Flayman, Barry's best friend.

"Can you believe it?" Adam burst out excitedly. "This is it!"

"I cannot believe it," Barry replied. "It's unbelievable."

"I'll see you there," Adam said. "Don't be late, OK?"

"I won't," Barry promised. "Bye."

He went over to his closet, trying to decide which

sweater to wear. On such an important day, it was a big decision, even though all the sweaters looked exactly alike—bright yellow with black stripes.

"Barry!" Janet Benson yelled up from the kitchen. "Are you ready yet?"

"Uh . . . almost, Mom!" he called back. He yanked a sweater down over his round bee tummy and then slipped on his tennis shoes. "I'm coming!"

He flew into the kitchen, where his parents were eating breakfast.

Mrs. Benson eyed his outfit critically through her glasses. "I thought you were going to wear the other sweater," she said.

"This *is* the other one," Barry said. "They're all the same anyway, Mom—remember?"

His mother pointed to the pile of honey pancakes on the table. "You want some honey on your honey?"

He shook his head. "I think I'll just have the honey."

Mr. Benson helped himself to a few pancakes. "Mmm . . . good honey," he told his wife. Then he looked over at Barry. "You know, son, we're very proud of you today."

"*Very* proud," Mrs. Benson echoed.

"Are you sure you can't come?" Barry asked them hopefully.

"We'd love to," his mother started to say. "But . . ."

"We're too busy," his father chimed in.

Barry nodded, knowing it was true. The honeybees in his hive could never get a day off from work.

"OK." He gulped down some honey, then wiped his mouth. "I'll see you later. Bye!"

With that, he leaped off the terrace—and flew down into the beehive toward his destiny. Today was graduation day—he was finally going to enter the real world and become a working honeybee.

Barry raced through the bustling streets and narrow alleyways of New Hive City. Finally, he spotted a podium that was set up outdoors in front of rows and rows of chairs. A large sign read: WELCOME, GRADUATES!

Barry zipped up the aisle, ducking into line behind Adam. The other bee wore a shirt and tie. He had frameless glasses on, too.

Adam grinned at him. "Well, if it isn't Barry B. Benson, college graduate!" he said.

"Not yet," Barry reminded his friend. "Did your parents come?"

"Nope," Adam answered.

"Too busy," the boys said together.

"I'm pretty excited," Barry said. "Can you believe that after today, *we're* going to be the ones who make the honey in this hive?"

"It's very cool," Adam agreed. "I can't wait to touch that stuff!"

Dean Buzzwell stood at the podium. "Welcome, New Hive City graduating class of"—he glanced at the clock—"nine-fifteen!"

There were so many bees in New Hive City that graduation was happening all the time.

"Congratulations," Dean Buzzwell went on. "And that concludes our graduation ceremonies!"

Barry joined in with the other bees in his class as they tossed their caps into the air. Like magic, their graduation caps were instantly replaced with work helmets.

"And so begins your career at Honex Industries!" Dean Buzzwell continued.

"Wow . . . ," Barry murmured. "That was fast. Do you think we'll actually get to do anything today?" he asked Adam.

"No." Adam shook his head. "Day one is just ori-entation."

A few minutes later the graduates were ushered onto a tram for a tour of Honex Industries. The Honex factory was the core of the beehive.

"Keep your hands and antennae inside the car at all times!" said the woman who was leading the tour. "My name is Trudy, and I'll be your guide today."

"I wonder what it's going to be like to work at Honex," Barry said nervously.

"It's a little scary," Adam said. "I mean, we're not kids anymore, you know."

In front of them, several doors slid open, one after the other, to let the tram through. Finally they were inside the lobby.

"Welcome to Honex, a division of Honesco, and a part of the Hexagon Group," Trudy announced proudly.

"Wow. . . ." Barry looked around, amazed that he was finally here. "This is it, Adam. We've arrived!"

"Now," Trudy said to the graduates, "we know that you, as a bee, have worked your whole life to get to this point so that you can work for your whole life. Congratulations!" She went on, "You won't ever work anywhere else—or do anything else—ever again!"

"Like I'd want to," Barry whispered.

"Yeah," Adam agreed. "Like, where are we going to go?"

"Nowhere," Barry replied with a grin. "We're here, baby!"

CHAPTER TWO

Barry paid close attention as Trudy explained the honey-making procedure to the new graduates.

"Honey production, of course, is an eighteen-step process," she began. "Honey begins as nectar. Our valiant pollen jocks bring it to the hive, where it's loaded into the Nec-tankers, and deposited into heating vats, which are then cooled and reheated fifty-eight thousand times before going through our exclusive triple filtering system." She pointed to a bunch of machines. "The machine is centrifuged at three million RPM, because, well, it's fun to do that."

All the bees on the tram laughed.

"To maintain our world-famous consistency, our honey is dropped onto belt pullers and manipulated over and over again until we simply can't take it anymore. Finally, it's color corrected, scent adjusted, and bubble contoured into this." She grabbed a test tube of honey from a technician who was working nearby, and held it up.

"This soothing, sweet syrup with its distinctive golden glow, which you all know as—"

"Honey!" the graduates called out together.

"And if every bee in the hive works hard every single day, we have just enough to survive as a species," she finished.

Trudy tossed the test tube into the crowd, and they all scrambled to get it.

A girl bee reached it first.

"She's pretty," Adam whispered to Barry.

Barry gave him a look. "She's my cousin," he said.

"She is?" Adam said, surprised.

"Duh!" Barry said, reminding him that all bees in a hive are related. "We're *all* cousins."

"Oh, oh, right," Adam murmured. "Of course."

Just then their tram passed a huge, clear storage tank with markings to indicate the amount of honey inside. Barry noticed that the honey was up to the one-cup line.

"Now this is going to impress you," Trudy announced. "We produce about two cups of honey every year."

"Wow," Barry said. "Two cups!"

"That is a load," remarked Adam.

"We would have produced three cups last year," Trudy said with a sigh, "if it hadn't been for those kids attacking us with that wiffle-ball bat. But we gave them a stinging they won't soon forget," she went on. "We lost a few men, but it was worth it, let me tell you."

She pointed ahead of the tram. "Now, over there you'll see our brand-new technology. We call it the Krelman."

Barry eyed the sleek-looking machine. "What does that do?" he asked curiously.

"It catches the little strand of honey that hangs down after you pour it. It saves us millions!" she explained.

The young bees watched the Krelman's mechanical fingers scoop up a drop of honey.

"Cool invention," someone said.

Adam shot up his hand. "Can anyone work on the Krelman?" he asked eagerly.

"Of course." Trudy nodded. "All bees are free to work in any field they choose."

Everyone cheered.

"And the good news is," Trudy went on, "you'll stay in that field—in the very job you pick—for the rest of your life."

For the rest of your life? Barry thought.

"At Honex, we constantly strive to improve every aspect of bee existence," Trudy was saying. "In fact, we . . ."

Barry poked Adam. "Did she just say you could only have one job for the rest of your life?" he whispered.

Adam nodded.

Barry ran a hand through the fuzz on his head. "I didn't know that," he murmured. "I thought . . ."

"For example," Trudy was saying, pointing to a stunt bee in a helmet who was getting hit with a newspaper again and again. "That bee is stress-testing our new helmet technology."

Next the stunt bee got hit in the helmet with a flyswatter, and after that, with a shoe. When he got back on his feet, he flashed them a thumbs-up.

The graduates clapped for him.

"I'm not sure that's the job for me," Barry murmured.

"And for you bees who worry about having too much time on your hands," Trudy said, "you'll be happy to know that bees, as a species, haven't had one day off in twenty-seven million years."

"So Honex will just work us to death!" joked Adam.

"We'll surely try!" Trudy replied, laughing.

The tram passed another large group of workers. Barry stared at them.

What if I don't like the job I choose? he thought. *What if it's boring? Or tiring, or—*

Just then the tram dropped steeply, plunging down a slope like a roller-coaster.

"Whooo!" the bees cried out in delight. They rocketed around the track and then sailed into the lobby, stopping at the very spot where their tour had begun.

"Whoa! That was awesome!" one bee cried. "I want to go on that ride again!"

"That blew my mind!" Adam said.

"Mine, too," Barry said. But he wasn't talking about the tram ride.

They climbed out of the tram car.

"So we graduate," he said to Adam, "and five minutes later, I have to decide what I'm going to do for the rest of my life? Is that what she was saying?"

"Yep, and then we're finished," Adam confirmed. "We're lucky because there's no anxiety, no doubt about our futures. Everything's decided. It's a load off my mind."

Barry looked at him. "Is it possible that, well, maybe I could stop and think about my future for a second?" he asked.

"Sure, go ahead." Adam looked at his watch. "OK. Time's up," he said a second later. "That's it, Barry," he said, clapping him on the back. "I've got news for you, buddy. For the rest of your life, you're a bee, making honey."

CHAPTER THREE

After the Honex tour was over, Barry walked with Adam along the street in downtown New Hive City. Brightly colored cars whizzed by. Above them rose the walls of the beehive, dotted with the terraces of bee homes.

"Adam," Barry said, "do you ever think that things work a little *too* well around here?"

Adam looked at him as if he were crazy. "Barry, how can things work too well? Bees have the most perfectly functioning society on earth."

"I don't feel like I'm functioning perfectly," Barry mumbled. He watched a bee fill his red car's gas tank from a honey pump.

"Please clear the gate!" a voice suddenly boomed. "Royal Nectar Force on approach! I repeat, Royal Nectar Force on approach!"

Barry looked up. Four large patrol bees were flying in through the hive's giant entrance. They wore cool-looking fighter-pilot jackets and helmets with visors.

"Hey! Check it out, Adam!" Barry exclaimed. "Those are pollen jocks—the bees who bring the nectar back to the hive!"

"Awesome!" Adam said. "I've never seen them up close like this."

"Me neither," Barry said. "Now that's a cool job!" he went on. "Pollen jocks know what it's like to go outside the hive."

"Yes," Adam reminded him, "but some of them don't come back."

A small crowd had gathered around the pollen jocks. Several young girl bees were shrieking and jumping up and down with excitement.

Barry watched closely. Each pollen jock had his own pit crew that removed the jock's backpack and loaded it onto a truck headed into Honex.

A bee who seemed to be their supervisor rushed over. "You guys did great! You're monsters! Sky freaks!" he told the pollen jocks.

"I wonder where those guys have just been," Barry said.

Adam shrugged. "Who knows."

"I mean, their day isn't planned," Barry went on.

"They're outside the hive all day long, flying who-knows-where, doing who-knows-what. . . ."

"Maybe you should be a pollen jock, Barry," Adam suggested.

"Yeah, right," Barry retorted. "All I've got to do is grow to twice my height and put on seventy grams of sinewy, rock-hard muscle."

"OK. You can't do that," Adam said.

"No. I can't," Barry agreed with a sigh. The pollen jocks waved good-bye to their fans and headed off. As they passed over Barry and Adam, pollen drifted down, dusting them both.

"Look at this stuff!" Barry exclaimed. "It's more pollen than you or I will ever see in our lifetimes."

Adam shrugged. "It's just a status symbol, Barry. It doesn't mean anything."

"You're right," Barry said. "It doesn't mean any-thing."

Just then two girl bees walked past.

"Hi!" they greeted Adam and Barry.

"Hi," Barry replied.

The girls giggled.

"You two seem kind of small for pollen jocks," one called over her shoulder.

Barry turned to Adam. "Did you see that?" he said. "They were laughing at us!"

Adam nodded. "Hey," he called out. "Have you

girls ever seen anyone do an impression of a fly?"

"No. . . ." Barry groaned. "Don't do the fly, Adam. Nobody likes flies. They're disgusting."

Nearby, a few pollen jocks named Jackson, Buzz, and Splitz were watching Barry and Adam.

"Look at those two," Jackson said, laughing.

"They're a couple of Hive Harrys," Splitz remarked.

"Come on," Jackson said a minute later. "Let's go have some fun."

The pollen jocks swaggered over to where Adam and Barry were still talking to the girls.

"Little gusty out there today, wasn't it, comrades?" asked Buzz.

"Yeah, gusty," Barry mumbled.

"We're going to hit a sunflower patch about six miles from here tomorrow," Buzz bragged.

"Wow!" The girls looked at him in awe. "That is so cool!" one said.

"You guys are so brave!" chimed in the other.

Barry glared at the pollen jocks. "Six miles from here, huh?"

"Barry," Adam said warningly, "don't—"

"That's right," Buzz said. "It's a puddle jump for us . . . but"—he looked Barry up and down—"I don't think you're up for it."

"Maybe I am," Barry blurted out.

"You are not!" Adam whispered loudly.

"We're departing at oh nine hundred hours, at J-Gate," Splitz informed them.

"OK. See you at J-Gate," Barry said nervously. He looked at Adam. "We'll be there."

"You know, I would really love to go," Adam spoke up, "but I had planned on not being dead tomorrow, and being dead would throw a bit of a wrench into my schedule—because I WOULD BE DEAD ALL DAY!"

The pollen jocks laughed loudly.

Then Splitz looked at Barry. "See you tomorrow," he said with a grin.

Barry nodded, then swallowed hard. *Yikes!* he thought. *What in the world have I gotten myself into?*

"Honex!"

Later that day, Barry stood outside on his family's balcony when someone came up from behind and tickled him.

Barry jumped. "Dad! You surprised me!"

Mr. Benson smiled at him. "What a day, huh, kid?" he said. "Have you decided what you're interested in yet? Viscosity? Heating and cooling? Pouring?"

"Well . . . ," Barry said slowly, "there sure are a lot of choices."

"But you only get one," his father reminded him.

Barry took a deep breath. "Do you ever get bored doing the same thing every day, Dad?" he blurted out. "You've been a stirrer forever."

"Son, let me tell you something about stirring a stick," Mr. Benson began. "The subtleties are infinite. The swirl, the curve of the ellipse . . . I've been there at Honex for twenty years, and I still get the chills." He showed Barry his biceps. "You don't get these guns in the Viscosity Department!"

"I don't know, Dad . . . ," Barry said. "The more I think about it, the more doubts I have. Maybe the honey field just isn't right for me."

"Really?" His father gave him a long look. "And you were thinking of what instead? Deep-sea fishing?"

"Well, no," Barry tried to explain, "I—"

"There's only honey, son!" Mr. Benson cut in. "It's who we are." He gestured around them at New Hive City bathed in a golden glow. "This is all honey. You're honey, I'm honey, your mother's honey." Then he yelled to Barry's mother. "Janet! Your son's not sure if he wants to go into the honey business!"

Barry's mother came out to the terrace carrying

drinks. From their terrace Barry could see every other bee family's terrace lining the walls of the hive. There were hundreds of terraces, all exactly the same.

"Oh, Barry," she said, smiling fondly at him. "You're so funny sometimes!"

"I'm not trying to be funny, Mom!" he insisted.

"You're not funny," Mr. Benson said. "You're going into honey." He held up his glass. "To honey!"

Mrs. Benson raised hers, too. "To honey!" she chimed in.

Other bees on nearby terraces joined in the toast. "To honey!" they declared.

Barry kept his eyes on the floor as he lifted his glass. "To honey ...," he echoed, his voice so soft no one could even hear him.

CHAPTER FOUR

"Hey, did you hear about Frankie?" Adam asked the next day. Barry was sitting in the passenger seat of Adam's red convertible. They were on their way to Honex to start their first day of work.

"Yeah, I heard about him," Barry replied.

"Are you going to his funeral?" asked Adam.

"No. I'm not going to his funeral," Barry replied. "Everybody knows that if you sting someone, you die. You don't waste it on a squirrel!" Barry shook his head. "Frankie was such a hothead."

"Yeah," Adam agreed. "I mean, he could have just gotten out of the way."

Suddenly, the road curled into a giant loop-the-loop.

"Whoa . . . Whooo!" the boys called out.

"I love how they incorporate an amusement park

right into our regular day," Adam exclaimed. "It's so much fun!"

Barry sighed. "I guess that's why they say we don't need vacations."

They pulled up in front of Honex and headed inside to the Job Placement Department.

A bee named Buzzwell sat at the counter. Behind him was a board that listed job openings at all the departments of Honex.

"Is it still available?" a bee named Sandy Shrimpkin asked.

"Hang on," Buzzwell told her. He looked at the numbers swiftly changing on the board. "There are two positions left. One of them is yours, Sandy. Congratulations!"

"Yeah!" Sandy cheered.

"What did you get?" Adam asked her.

"I got the job picking out the crud!" Sandy said. "It's so stellar!"

"Wow," Adam replied. "Cool."

Buzzwell looked at Adam and Barry. "Couple of newbies?" he asked.

"Yes, sir. Our first day," said Adam. "And we are ready!"

"Well, step up and make your choice," Buzzwell said. "The honey's dripping."

Barry stared at the board.

HEATING, COOLING, VISCOSITY, KRELMAN, POLLEN COUNTING, STUNT BEE, POURING, STIRRER.

Those were his choices.

"Do you want to go first?" asked Adam.

"No." Barry shook his head. "You go."

Adam looked at Buzzwell. "Any chance of getting onto the Krelman?" he asked hopefully.

Buzzwell peered at him. "Do you ever get motion sickness?" he asked. "Because the Krelman workers do spin around quite a bit."

"Oh . . . OK. . . ." Adam looked back up at the board, thinking.

"Sorry about that," Buzzwell said suddenly. "I see that the Krelman just closed out. There are no more job opportunities there at the moment."

"Oh!" Adam said, disappointed. "Bummer."

"But we do have plenty of positions in Pouring," Buzzwell told him.

On the board, the Krelman suddenly went from CLOSED to OPEN.

"And the Krelman just opened up again!" Buzzwell declared.

"What happened?" asked Adam.

"Whenever a bee dies, there's an opening," Buzzwell explained. "At Honex, nothing stays open or closed for very long."

This is so depressing, Barry thought.

For the rest of his life, he would be stuck pouring or stirring or cooling honey. He'd never get to see the world outside the hive.

Adam was still gazing at the board, trying to make up his mind. "This is so hard," he murmured. "Barry, what do you want to . . . Barry? Barry?"

But Barry couldn't hear him. He had flown away.

At the J-Gate, the pollen jocks were going through final preflight checks. Barry stood off to the side, watching them for a few minutes.

"All right, we've got the sunflower patch in quadrant nine," one confirmed.

Barry felt his antennae vibrate. "Hello?" he answered.

It was Adam. "What happened to you?" he demanded. "I turned around and you were gone!"

"I'm going out," Barry whispered to him.

"You're going out!" Adam echoed. "Out where?"

"Out there," Barry replied.

"Oh, no." Adam realized where Barry was. "You're not."

"Oh, yes, I am," Barry said. "It's a one-time thing. I'm going to try it."

"Barry. You're going to die!" Adam said. "You are psychotic! Crazy! Don't do it. You'll—"

Adam was still ranting when Barry clicked off the antenna phone. He made his way over to the pollen jocks, who were getting final instructions from the supervisor.

"If anyone is feeling brave," Lou Duva was saying, "there's a Korean deli on Eighty-third Street that gets their roses today."

"Hey, guys!" Barry waved.

They looked up.

"Well, look at that!" exclaimed Buzz.

"Isn't that the kid we saw yesterday?" asked Splitz.

Lou Duva put out an arm to block Barry's path. "Hold it right there, son!" he ordered. "The flight deck is restricted."

"It's OK, Lou," said Jackson. "We're going to take him up and see what he can do."

Splitz and Buzz laughed loudly.

"Really?" said Lou Duva, giving Barry another look.

A small bee ran up with some papers for Barry to sign.

"Sign here," the bee said. "Just initial that. Thank you. This releases us from all responsibility for whatever happens to you."

"OK," Lou Duva announced. "We've got a rain advisory today, and as you all know, bees cannot fly in rain. So keep your eyes on the sky. As always."

He glanced down at his clipboard. "And watch out for other hazards—your brooms, your hockey sticks, dogs, birds, bears, and bats. Also, I got a new warning here. There have been a couple of reports of root beer being poured on us, and some kind of cooking spray. Murphy's in a home now because of it. He's out of his mind. He can't stick to anything."

"That's awful," Barry said. He sure hoped nothing like that happened to him out there.

"And, of course," Lou Duva went on in a solemn voice, "for any of you going out for the first time, there is absolutely, positively, no talking to humans."

"Excuse me!" Barry raised his hand. "Why is that so important?"

"We've got nothing to say to them," Buzz replied.

"And we don't want to hear what they have to say, either," Splitz chimed in.

"All right, jocks! Launch positions!" Lou Duva called out.

Splitz looked at Barry. "Are you sure you're ready for this, hotshot?" he asked.

"Yeah. Yeah, bring it on," Barry replied, acting brave.

The pollen jocks prepared for flight.

"Wind, check!" shouted Buzz.

"Antennae, check!" shouted another guy.

"Wings, check!" said Jackson.

"Stinger, check!" said Splitz.

"OK, then, crew, let's move it out!" Lou Duva called.

They all flipped down their visors. Then the bees from the pit crew cranked the pollen jocks' wings and removed the starting blocks. Soon a loud humming sound filled the air.

"Pound those petunias, you striped stem suckers!" Lou Duva ordered. "All of you, drain those flowers! You hear me? Drain those flowers!"

A flight-deck worker crouched low, using hand signals to steer the bees through an archway that led out of the hive. Barry followed them all, not quite sure of what he was doing.

And then before he quite realized what was happening, they were out—out of the hive and flying toward a bright blue sky that seemed to stretch on forever.

CHAPTER FIVE

"Whoa!" Barry gasped as the bees climbed high above treetops in formation.

"I'm out!" he exclaimed. "I'm out of the hive!"

Below him was a colorful wonderland of trees, flowers, green grass, and blue ponds. The outside world seemed so . . . big! The bees flew over some people riding bicycles, and then approached a path lined with brightly colored flowers.

Splitz spoke into a radio. "This is Blue Leader. We have a roses visual. Bring it around thirty degrees and hold."

"Roses," Barry echoed, taking in the sight of the colorful flowers. "They're beautiful."

"Thirty degrees, roger," Jackson answered Splitz. "Bringing it around."

Barry watched as a bunch of pollen jocks broke off from the main group. Their job, it seemed, was to go and collect nectar from the roses.

He flew down to get a better look.

"Stand to the side," a jock told him. "This equipment has got a bit of a kick."

The jock had a nectar pump. He fired several tubes into the flower. Then the machine jumped as he started it up. The pump began sucking nectar up the tubes, and filled a glass chamber.

"What a machine that is!" Barry commented.

"Have you ever seen pollination up close?" the jock asked him.

Barry shook his head.

"Watch this," the jock said.

He took off and Barry followed, watching as pollen dust fell to the ground below. Instantly, flowers bloomed to life.

"Whoa," Barry exclaimed. "That's amazing!"

He shot upward, rejoining the jocks in the sky. They swooped low over a pond, grazing the surface. Then they zipped back up into the air.

Buzz was talking into his radio. "I'm picking up a lot of bright yellow—could be daisies. Don't we need those?"

"Copy that," Splitz replied.

Barry looked down, where he saw a green field dotted with something that was round and yellow.

The bees went into a deep bank and dove toward the target.

"Hold on!" Buzz shouted suddenly. "One of those flowers seems to be on the move!"

"Say again?" Splitz said. "Are you reporting a *moving* flower?"

"Affirmative!" said Buzz.

The pollen jocks continued their descent and landed on the green field. Nearby, two humans were holding things that looked to Barry like sticks with nets.

"That was on the line!" the man was saying in an annoyed tone.

Splitz looked confused as he bent over one of the round yellow objects. "This is definitely not a flower," he said. "But what is it?"

"I don't know," said Jackson, "but I'm loving the color."

Splitz leaned closer and sniffed. "It smells good. Not like a flower. But I like it."

"It's fuzzy, too!" Jackson added.

Buzz took a sniff. "It smells funny to me—like chemicals or something."

Barry collapsed on top of one of the round yellow things. "Oh, my gosh!" he declared in exhaustion.

Jackson snarled at him. "Hey, candy brain, get off of there!"

Barry tried to pull off his legs, but they had stuck fast.

"Problem!" he called out.

Just then a human reached down and scooped up the yellow globe—with Barry on it.

"Guys!" he yelled in a panic.

"Oh, no," Buzz murmured. "This could be bad."

"Affirmative," Splitz declared.

"I've got another tennis ball, Ken!" the human called out to her companion. She had brown hair cut in a bob.

Barry swallowed hard. *So that's what this is,* he realized, *a tennis ball.*

The pollen jocks hadn't landed in a field; they'd landed on a tennis court!

The woman crossed the court, bouncing the ball with Barry on it. Each time it hit the ground, the other bees gasped loudly.

Barry held his breath as the ball went up and down. "Very close . . . ," he murmured. "This is going to hurt—Mama's little boy is going to get hurt. . . ."

"You are way out of position, rookie," Splitz called to Barry.

Like I don't already know that, he thought.

Suddenly, the woman tossed the ball high into the air.

"Oh, no!" Barry cried as it dropped down in front of her and she slammed it with the racket in her other hand. The ball shot across the wide net toward the opposite side of the court.

"Hey, Vanessa!" her opponent, Ken, yelled. "I'm coming at you like a missile!" Sure enough, he fired the ball back across the net. Ken was tall with dark hair and a prominent chin.

Barry felt g-forces as he rocketed back and forth through the air.

"Whoa!" he yelled to the pollen jocks. "Help me!"

They watched helplessly as Vanessa hit the ball back hard in a high, arcing lob.

Ken ran up to meet the ball, a killer look in his eyes. "You can just start packing up, honey, because I believe you're about to eat it!"

A pollen jock finally decided to do something. From the sideline, Jackson tried to get Ken's attention.

"Ahem," Jackson said.

Ken was distracted and turned toward the sound. The ball hit the edge of the tennis racket, and Barry screamed as the ball bounced out of the tennis court, and onto the street. It hit a big umbrella that was shielding a hot dog cart, then sailed into the middle of the street.

Finally, after bouncing around a few more times, the ball stuck in the front grille of a huge car.

Barry felt himself tumble off the ball and get sucked through a long black tunnel. All around him were whirling metal vanes and clanging pistons.

"Ahhhhhhhh! Ohhhhhh!" he screamed as the car's air-conditioning blasted him. "It's cold in here!" Beside him was a frozen grasshopper.

The next thing Barry knew, he was sucked inside the passenger compartment of the car with a family.

He bumped into the mother's magazine.

"Aagghh!" she screamed. "There's a bee in the car!"

A grandmother and little boy started yelling, too.

Uh-oh, Barry thought. He bounced around inside the car, desperately looking for a way out.

"Kill it!" the mother yelled at her husband. "Do something!"

"I'm driving!" the father shot back.

Barry flew past a little girl, who was strapped into a car seat.

She waved at him. "Hi, bee!" she said.

"He's back here!" the little boy shouted to his parents. "The bee's back here—and he's going to sting me!"

The car swerved along the road. Barry zipped into the back, right into a large crate, where a slobbery dog snapped at him. Dodging all around, Barry barely managed to avoid the dog's jaws and his flying spittle.

"Nobody move," the mother ordered. "If you don't move, he won't sting you."

The grandmother reached into her bag and pulled out a can of nonstick cooking spray.

"Little varmint!" she said. "I'll nonstick-cook and spray him!"

Barry gasped. He remembered what Lou Duva had told him about the danger of cooking spray.

The grandmother removed the cap and aimed the nozzle at Barry.

"Fry him, Granny!" The little boy egged her on. "Get him good!"

"Mom!" said the mother. "Is that really—"

"Be quiet! I'm busy back here," the grandmother snapped.

The dad looked annoyed. "Can't you control your mother?" he snapped at his wife.

Granny was scanning the car, trying to locate Barry. "Stick to this, bee!" she growled. "I'll mess you up!"

"Kill it, Mom!" the mother called.

As Barry zigzagged through the car, Grandma kept trying to blast him. Soon all the car windows—and the father's glasses—were covered with cooking spray.

"Watch out!" the mother screamed as the car swerved dangerously.

The father lost control of the car and sideswiped a couple of other cars.

Barry landed on the car's TV screen.

The boy spotted him. "I've got him now!" he yelled. He flipped up the TV screen, catapulting Barry into the back with the dog again.

The mother was going crazy. "Get it! Get it!" she screamed.

Frantic, Barry flew all over the car.

There's got to be some way out of here, he thought. He bounced around on the control panel and then finally got lucky. He hit the switch that opened the sunroof and flew right out of the car.

CHAPTER SIX

"Whew!" Barry let out a sigh of relief as he flew along the street. "This is one weird, wild hive," he decided. "I've got to get home."

He had no idea where the tennis courts were—or where the pollen jocks had gone, for that matter.

As he cruised around, trying to figure out how to get back to New Hive City, he felt a raindrop.

Oh, no, he thought nervously. *I can't fly in the rain.*

More drops fell.

For a few minutes, Barry was able to dodge the rain. But then it started pouring.

"Mayday! Mayday!" he called. "Bee going down!"

He glanced around, trying to find a shelter. He shot toward a colorful flower box on a window ledge outside a tall apartment building. Shivering and exhausted, he landed on the ledge, then crawled inside an open window. He shook himself off like a dog.

A second later, four humans walked into the apartment.

"Ken, can you close the window, please?" a woman called.

"Sure, Vanessa," he answered.

Barry ducked behind the drapes. "Oh, no, more humans," he moaned. "I don't need this!"

Ken came over to close the window. Barry didn't see him lower the glass pane because the bee was hiding in the curtains. Once Ken moved away, Barry poked his head out.

These are the people from the tennis court, Barry realized.

The humans sat down. There were two women and two men.

"So what's this new job?" the other man asked Ken.

"Artificial diamonds, Andy," he replied. "I'm going to sell them."

"Really?" Andy said.

"Yep." Ken nodded. "They're called Ziamoniques."

Barry wanted to escape before the people spotted him. He hovered in the air near the top of the window and then launched himself forward.

"Ow!" he cried, striking something hard. "What was that?" He tried again and again, but each time he hit his nose. He couldn't see that there was a clear glass windowpane in his way.

Finally, he gave up and jumped onto the drapes again.

The men were still talking about the fake diamonds.

"So even a jeweler can't tell the difference?" asked Andy.

"Well, certainly, *you* couldn't tell," Ken replied.

"And what kind of sizes do these stones come in?" Andy wanted to know.

"Three cuts," Ken informed him. "Walnut, ambassador, and juggernaut."

"What's the walnut?" asked Andy.

"It's kind of round and bumpy—appropriate for a first marriage," Ken said. "The diamonds were developed for astronauts' wives."

Still looking for a way out, Barry spotted something glowing in the middle of the ceiling. "Oh!" he cried happily. "There's the sun! Maybe that's the way out."

He zoomed up, heading straight for the glowing object. "Hmmm . . ." he murmured, drawing closer. "I don't remember the sun having a big number seventy-five on it!"

Barry slammed hard into a lightbulb. Knocked

silly, he tumbled down into a bowl of guacamole that was sitting on the coffee table.

Andy dipped a chip into the bowl, scooping up guacamole—and a bee.

Oh, boy! Barry thought as the chip traveled closer to the guy's mouth.

"So they're guaranteed?" Andy asked Ken.

"Oh, yes," Ken replied. "If the stone falls out of the setting, we'll replace it for free for up to seventeen months.

"You should see how they churn these babies out," Ken went on. "They're going to be huge!"

Barry perched on the chip, frozen as Andy lifted it higher and higher.

Good-bye, Mom. Good-bye, Dad, he thought. *Thanks for everything. . . .*

"Wait, Andy!" Ken shouted. *"Beeeeeee!"*

Andy dropped the chip and jumped up onto the sofa.

Ken ran toward Barry, carrying two huge boots. "Stand back!" he ordered. "These are winter boots!"

"Wait!" The woman named Vanessa raced into the room. "Don't kill it!" she shouted at Ken.

Barry let out his breath. *Whew!*

"Vanessa." Ken looked at her. "You know I'm allergic to bees. This thing could kill me."

She picked up a glass and gently placed it over Barry. Then she looked back at Ken. "Why does his life have any less value than yours?"

"Why does his life have any less value than mine?" Ken shot back at her. "Is that what you're saying?"

"I'm just saying, all life has value," Vanessa replied. "You don't know what he's capable of feeling. He's probably terrified right now."

Bingo! Barry thought. He shuddered, thinking about what might have just happened to him.

Vanessa picked up the brochure that Ken had been showing Andy. She ripped off a page, then slid it under the glass.

"My brochure," Ken murmured wistfully. "She just destroyed my brochure!"

Barry kept his eyes on Vanessa as she carried him over to the window. She lifted the glass pane to open it. She smiled at Barry, and blinked her big green eyes.

"There you go, little guy," she said softly. "You're free now."

"I'm not scared of bees or anything," Ken was saying to the other lady and Andy. "It's just . . . you know, an allergic thing."

"Aren't you allergic to dogs, too?" asked Andy.

"What are you, a vet, now?" asked Ken.

"No, I'm not a vet," Andy replied. "I . . ."

Outside it was still raining. Barry huddled on a leaf in the flower box, unable to go anywhere.

Before long, he could hear the humans inside saying good-bye to each other.

"So, Vanessa, how's this weekend?" asked Ken. "Do you want to go out on another date?"

"Uh . . ." Vanessa hesitated. "Maybe, Ken," she said at last. "I'll let you know."

"OK, bye-bye, then," Ken answered.

"Bye." She closed the door behind them.

Barry felt himself relax a little. He still couldn't go home in the rain, but at least he knew that Vanessa wouldn't try to pulverize him.

He watched her pick up some dishes and carry them into the kitchen.

I've got to say something to her, he thought. *I mean, she saved my life.*

Then he remembered Lou Duva's command to the pollen jocks.

I know we're not supposed to talk to people, he told himself, *but if it wasn't for her, I wouldn't be here right now.*

Barry flew back into the apartment. In the kitchen he landed on a shelf and hid behind a can of tuna fish.

Maybe I'd better not talk to her, he thought. *I could really get into trouble.*

But she saved my life, he remembered a minute

later. *Where are my manners? I've got to do it.*

He stood there for a few more minutes, trying to make up his mind. *No ... yes ... I can't do it. ... I've got to do it ... How should I start talking to her? "Do you like jazz?" No, that's no good. ... I know what to say—"I love your hair!" No, that's not right. ...*

Vanessa walked by, carrying a stack of dishes. Barry took a deep breath. "Ummm ... hi ... ," he blurted out.

"*Aaagh!*" Vanessa shrieked, dropping the dishes that were in her arms. She hopped back, away from Barry.

"Sorry!" he called. "Sorry about that!"

Vanessa stared at him, blinking in surprise. "You're talking!" she exclaimed.

"Yes." Barry nodded. "I'm talking."

"You're talking!" she repeated. "Oh, my gosh ... you're a bee—and you're talking!"

"I know. ..." He fumbled for words. "I'm sorry. I'm so sorry about scaring you like that."

"It's OK. It's fine," Vanessa reassured him. "It's just ... I know I'm dreaming, but I don't remember going to bed or anything."

"I'm sure this is all very disconcerting," Barry said.

"Well, yes it is," Vanessa agreed. "I mean, you're a bee."

"I am definitely a bee," Barry replied. "And you

know, I'm not supposed to be doing this, but they were all trying to kill me, and if it wasn't for you . . ." He took a deep breath. "I had to thank you. It's just the way I was raised."

Vanessa picked up a fork and jabbed herself hard in the hand. "Ow!"

Barry watched her, confused. "That was a little weird."

"I must be dreaming," she told herself. "This can't be real. I can't be talking to a bee."

"Anyway," Barry said softly. "I—"

"And a bee is talking to me," Vanessa went on. "We're having a conversation."

"I just want you to know that I'm grateful," Barry said. "And I'm going to leave now."

"Wait!" said Vanessa. "How did you learn how to do that?"

"Do what?" he asked.

"The talking thing," she said.

"Oh, I don't know," Barry replied. "The same way you learned to talk, I guess. 'Mama, Dada, honey . . .'" He shrugged. "You just pick it up."

"That's very funny," Vanessa said.

"Well, bees are funny," Barry informed her. "If we didn't laugh, we'd cry, with what we have to deal with."

Vanessa laughed, relaxing a little. "Can I, uh, get

you something?" she asked.

"Like what?" Barry wanted to know.

She shrugged. "I don't know. Coffee?"

"Well, I don't want to put you out or anything," he replied.

"It's no trouble," she told him.

"Unless you're making it anyway," he went on.

"It takes two minutes," Vanessa said.

"Really?" Barry said.

"It's just coffee," she answered.

"Actually, I would love a cup," he said.

"How about some cake?" she asked.

"I really shouldn't," he said, hesitating. He patted his round belly.

"Oh, have a little cake," she said. "One slice won't hurt you."

"I'm trying to lose a couple of micrograms here," Barry said. He pointed to his abdomen. "These stripes don't help."

He glanced over to where Vanessa was pouring coffee onto the floor.

"Are you OK?" Barry asked.

"No." She sank to her knees. "I'm definitely not OK."

CHAPTER
SEVEN

Barry finally managed to convince Vanessa that she wasn't dreaming. He was a real bee—and the two of them were really talking to each other.

After she'd cleaned up her kitchen, they went up to her rooftop terrace, which overlooked Central Park in New York City. Vanessa had a garden up there, where she was growing lots of flowers.

Barry perched on her keychain, sipping coffee and telling her about graduation and working at Honex.

"I don't know what to do," he went on. "I want to do my part for the hive, but I just can't do it the way they want."

"I know how you feel," Vanessa confessed.

He glanced at her. "You do?" he said.

"Sure." She nodded. "My parents wanted me to be a lawyer or a doctor, but I wanted to be a florist."

She pointed to the pretty garden nearby. "All my life, my only interest was flowers."

"That wouldn't have been a problem for my folks," Barry said. He looked out at the park and pointed. "See? There's my hive, right over there. You can see it from here."

Vanessa looked. "Oh, you live in the meadow," she said.

"Yes!" Barry exclaimed. "Do you know the turtle pond?"

"Yes," she answered with a smile.

"I'm right off of that," he told her excitedly.

"Oh, no way," Vanessa said. "I know that area really well."

"Really?" Barry asked.

Nearby on the roof, a maintenance man was fixing a vent. He looked up when he heard Vanessa talking—and then did a double take when he saw that she was alone. Of course, a bee was too tiny for the maintenance man to see.

"Are you all right, ma'am?" he called.

"Oh, yes, I'm fine," she answered. "I'm just having a couple cups of coffee over here."

"OK . . . ," the man said, still looking at her oddly. "Whatever you say."

Barry wiped his mouth. "Anyway, this has been great, Vanessa. Thanks for the coffee."

"No trouble," she replied.

"Sorry I couldn't finish it," he said. He looked at the crumb cake she'd put on a plate. "Can I take a piece with me?"

"Sure," she said. "Here, have a crumb. She took a crumb from her lip and held it out to him.

"Oh." Barry looked at her. "Thanks."

An awkward silence fell between them.

"OK, then," he said, unsure of what to do next. "I guess I'll see you around, or not, or maybe . . ."

She smiled at him. "OK, Barry."

"And thank you so much again, you know, for before," he added.

"Oh, that?" Vanessa said. "It was nothing."

"Well, I definitely wouldn't call saving my life nothing," he said, "But . . . anyway . . ."

Vanessa held out her finger, and Barry reached out to shake it.

The next morning, Barry found Adam at Honex Industries.

"It sounds amazing," Adam said after Barry told him about his adventure with the pollen jocks and the people outside the hive.

"Oh, it *was* amazing!" Barry gloated. "It was the scariest—and happiest—moment of my life."

"Humans!" Adam said. "I can't believe you were with humans—giant, scary humans! What were they like?"

"Huge and crazy," Barry told him. "They talk crazy and they eat crazy—giant things like crumb cake." He remembered the scene inside the car. "And they drive around real crazy, too!"

Adam wanted to know more. "Do they really try to kill bugs, the way they always do on TV?"

"Some of them do," Barry said. He thought about Vanessa. "But some of them don't. Some humans are really nice."

"How did you get back here?" Adam asked.

"Poodle," Barry said. "I rode a poodle all the way home."

"Well, you did it," Adam said. "And I'm glad. You saw whatever you wanted to see out there; you had your little 'experience.' And now that you're back, you can pick out your job, and everything can be normal again."

Barry kept his eyes down. "Well . . . actually . . ."

Adam glanced at him, alarmed. "Actually what?"

"I met someone," Barry blurted out.

"You met someone?" Adam echoed. "Barry . . . is she bee-ish?"

"Mmmm . . . er . . ." Barry stalled.

"She's not a wasp, is she?" Adam said. "Oh my

gosh. If she's a wasp, your parents will kill you!"

"No, no, no," Barry assured him. "She's not a wasp."

"A spider?" Adam guessed.

Barry shook his head. "I'm not attracted to spiders, Adam. I know lots of guys think they're really cool, with those eight legs and everything, but I just can't get past that face." He made an ugly spider face at Adam.

Beep, beep, beep.

"Wait a second, Barry," Adam said. "Hear that? I'm getting a fax."

Beep, beep, beep.

He squatted over a stack of fax paper and his stinger started scribbling out the fax.

"It's a junk fax," Adam realized. "Just a bunch of stupid menus." He stood up again. "So who is she?"

"She's a . . ." Barry paused. "A human."

"Oh, no. No. No." Adam shook his head over and over again. "Tell me this isn't happening. It's a bee law, Barry," he went on. "You wouldn't break a bee law."

"Her name is Vanessa," Barry said.

"Oh." Adam moaned. "Oh, boy!"

"She's *soooo* nice," Barry went on. "And get this— she's a florist!"

Adam was still shaking his head. "Oh, no. You're dating a human florist?"

"We're not dating," Barry admitted.

"You're flying outside the hive," Adam said. "You're talking to human beings who attack our homes!"

"She saved my life, Adam," Barry tried to explain. "And she understands me."

"This is over," Adam said firmly. "You've got to end this relationship, or else . . ."

Barry pulled out the crumb that Vanessa had given him. Before Adam could finish, he stuffed it into his friend's face.

"Oh . . . my . . . gosh . . ." Adam's face lit up as he tasted the sugary crumb. "What was that?"

"They call it a crumb," Barry told him.

Adam swooned. "That was so stinging stripey!"

"And that's not even what they eat," Barry went on eagerly. "That just falls off what they eat! Do you know what a cinnamon roll is?"

"No," Adam said.

"It's bread with cinnamon and frosting and . . ." Barry kept going. "And they heat it up and it's warm and delicious—"

"Be quiet!" Adam ordered him as they entered Adam's office at Honex. "Stop. Listen to me. We are not them. We're us. There's us and there's them."

Barry just stared at him.

"You have got to start thinking bee, my friend, thinking bee, OK?" Adam urged him. "I mean it."

"OK, thinking," Barry echoed. But he wasn't thinking about what Adam wanted him to think about.

Instead, his thoughts were all about Vanessa and leaving the hive again.

CHAPTER EIGHT

"**I** found him!" Barry's father called. "He's in the pool, Janet!"

Mrs. Benson hurried over. "Barry, what are you doing?"

It was three days later. Barry was lying on a raft in the hexagon-shaped honey pool, his legs dangling in the honey. The sun shone brightly over his head.

He peered up at his parents. "Think bee," he murmured. "I've got to be thinking bee. . . ."

"Barry!" Mr. Benson snapped impatiently. "How much longer is this going to go on? It's been three days. I don't understand why you're not working."

Barry drifted around lazily in the pool. "You know, Dad," he said with a sigh, "that job placement board is kind of intimidating. I mean, what's the difference between 'filtering' and 'picking out the crud'?"

His mother sighed. "Oh, Barry."

"To tell you the truth," Barry went on, "I'm enjoying my life the way it is right now."

"What life?" his father said. "You have no life! You have no job! You're barely a bee!"

"I'm a bee," Barry said.

"Bees make honey!" Mr. Benson said. "And guess what? You're not making any!"

"Would it kill you just to make a little?" Mrs. Benson chimed in.

Barry rolled off the raft. As he sank to the bottom of the pool, he could still hear his parents' voices, but now they were muffled.

Much better, he thought lazily.

"Barry, come out from under there!" his mother ordered him. "Your father is talking to you. Martin, would you talk to him, please?"

"Barry!" Mr. Benson snapped, peering down at his son through tinted glasses. "I'm talking to you!"

Barry let his thoughts wander far away. In his mind he pictured himself picnicking with Vanessa in a beautiful park. They ate some of that delicious human food together, and then she climbed into an ultra-light one-person plane painted black and yellow. The plane took off, and a second later, Barry was there beside her. The two of them flew through the sky side by side.

Aaaah, heaven, Barry thought.

"Watch this!" Vanessa said suddenly in his daydream. Her plane did a loop—and then flew right into the side of a mountain. It burst into a huge ball of flames.

"No!" Barry screamed. "Vanessa!"

His eyes flew open. He kicked hard to get back up to the top of the pool.

He panted for a few minutes, trying to catch his breath.

"It's OK," his father said soothingly. "We're still here."

"I told you not to yell at him, Martin," Mrs. Benson said. "He doesn't respond when you yell at him."

Mr. Benson spun toward her. "Well then why are you yelling at me?" he demanded.

"Because you don't listen," Mrs. Benson shot back.

"I'm certainly not listening to this," Mr. Benson said in a huff.

Barry climbed out of the pool and began toweling off.

His mother watched him put on his striped sweater.

"Sorry, Mom, I've got to go," he said.

"Where are you going?" she asked in a worried voice.

"Nowhere," Barry said. "I'm . . . uh . . . meeting a friend." With that, he jumped off the balcony and flew away.

"A girl?" his mother called after him. "Is this why you can't decide about work?"

"Is she bee-ish?" Mr. Benson yelled. "She'd better be bee-ish!"

Barry waved. "Bye! See you later!"

Mrs. Benson turned to her husband. "I just hope she's bee-ish," she murmured.

Barry flew straight to Vanessa's flower shop. In the window of her store, he spotted a poster announcing something called the Tournament of Roses Parade.

Barry headed into the shop and asked Vanessa about it.

She explained that it was a big parade, which had been held in Pasadena, California, every year since the 1800s.

"So they have a parade with motorized floats made of flowers?" he asked as they left the shop and walked down the street.

A dreamy expression crossed Vanessa's face. "It's not just a parade," she murmured. "The floats have flowers from all over the world, and they're elaborately decorated, almost like movie sets. It's every florist's dream to be in Pasadena that day—up on a float, surrounded by flowers, with crowds cheering. . . ." She sighed.

"Boy, that sounds like quite a scene," Barry said. "I'd love to hit that sometime, too."

Vanessa looked at him and then suddenly changed the subject. "I've got a question for you, Barry. How come you don't fly everywhere?"

"It's exhausting," Barry told her. "Why don't you humans run everywhere? Wouldn't that be much faster?"

"I get it." Vanessa nodded.

A lady passing by suddenly swatted at Barry.

So did a man carrying a briefcase. "Dumb bees!" he snapped.

Vanessa shot the man a nasty look.

"Barry," she said sympathetically, "it's hard to be a bee, isn't it? You must just want to sting all those jerks."

"We try really hard not to sting anyone," Barry told her. "It's usually fatal for us."

"I guess you have to watch your temper, then," Vanessa remarked.

"Oh, yeah, very carefully," Barry said as they entered a supermarket. "When you're mad, you do other stuff, like kick a wall, take a walk, write a letter. . . . You work through it like any other emotion—sadness, jealousy . . ."

Barry hopped on top of some cardboard boxes in the middle of an aisle. He didn't notice a stock boy standing nearby.

"Hey! A bee!" the guy cried. He grabbed a magazine and whacked Barry with it.

"Oh, my goodness!" Vanessa gasped. "Are you OK, Barry?"

"Yeah." Barry got to his feet shakily. "Whew. That was a close one."

Vanessa grabbed the magazine from the stock boy and hit him with it. "What's wrong with you?" she demanded.

The guy looked at her. "It's a bug, lady."

"Well, he's not bothering anybody," Vanessa said. "Get out of here, you creep." She pushed him away.

Barry tried to shake off the pain. "That must have been a circular from the Pick and Save," he said.

"It was." Vanessa looked at him, impressed. "How did you know that?"

"It felt like about ten pages," he explained. "Seventy-five pages is pretty much our limit. Anything thicker than that, and we're a pancake."

"Boy, you've really got that down to a science," Vanessa remarked.

"We have to know these things," Barry told her. "I lost a cousin to an Italian fashion magazine. Have you ever seen how big those things are?"

"They're huge," Vanessa agreed.

They strolled through the store. Soon they came to an enormous display packed with honey jars.

Barry froze. "What in the name of Mighty Hercules is this?" he burst out. "How did this get here?" He flew closer to the labels, reading the names out loud: "Cute Bee . . . Golden Blossom . . . Private Select . . ."

"Oh." Vanessa's turned to the honey display.

"Why is this here?" asked Barry.

"So that people can buy it," she said, as if it were obvious. "We *eat* honey, Barry."

"You what?" Barry couldn't believe it. "You eat it?" He waved a hand at all the shelves packed with food. "You mean to tell me that you people don't have enough food of your own?"

Vanessa looked flustered. "Well, yes, we—"

Barry cut her off. "How do you even get this honey?" he demanded.

"Well, bees make it," she said. "And—"

"I know who makes it!" Barry informed her. "And it's hard to make it! There's heating and cooling, and stirring, and filtering—you need a whole big Krelman thing."

"It's organic," Vanessa tried to explain.

"It's *our*-ganic!" Barry retorted.

"It's just honey, Barry," she said.

"It's just . . . what?" He was still in shock as he turned back to the honey display. "Bees don't know about this," he said. "It's stealing—a lot of stealing!"

Vanessa stared at him, speechless.

"You people have taken our homes, our schools, our hospitals," he went on. "Honey is all we have. And it's for sale? I'm going to get to the bottom of this!" he vowed.

With that, he zipped over to a jar of honey and ripped off the label.

CHAPTER NINE

Barry suddenly found himself with a mission. In the supermarket storeroom, he found a marker and blacked out his yellow stripes. Then he slapped some war paint onto his face. Barry approached the stock boy, who was unpacking boxes of honey jars.

He zoomed toward the stock boy's face and backed him against a wall. The guy's nametag read HECTOR.

"Who's your supplier?" Barry demanded.

Hector made a strangled sound.

"Tell me!" Barry ordered.

"Supplier?" Hector echoed. "You've got the wrong idea, bee! We were just about to return all this honey to the bees."

"Yeah, right," Barry growled. "Tell me another one!"

The boy reached over and grabbed a tiny pushpin from a nearby bulletin board. He held it out like a weapon in front of Barry's face.

"You're too late," the boy snarled. "It's our honey now!"

"Aha!" Barry cried. He turned and began fencing Hector's pushpin with his stinger. "You, sir, have crossed the wrong sword!"

"And, you, sir," Hector retorted, "will soon be in my butterfly collection!"

"Where is that honey coming from?" Barry demanded. He knocked the pushpin from the stock boy's hand, then put his stinger right up to Hector's nose. "Tell me where!"

It took only a second for him to confess everything.

"Honey Farms!" he blurted out. He pointed to a truck parked outside the grocery store. "The honey comes from Honey Farms. Please don't hurt me!"

Barry let him go, then zipped outside. The Honey Farms truck was just leaving the loading dock. He shot after the truck as it turned down a narrow alleyway. The truck splashed through a big puddle, soaking Barry and washing off the black marker that covered his stripes.

Barry followed the truck onto a busy street,

zigzagging past a bus and several cabs. Finally, he grabbed hold of a bicycle messenger's backpack. The bike sped along the crowded city street.

A few minutes later, the Honey Farms truck shot ahead. Barry grabbed a cord that was hanging from the backpack and used it like a slingshot to launch himself through the air. He landed right on the truck's windshield.

"Oh, my!" Barry gazed around in horror. Splattered across the glass were dozens of stiff bugs.

"What happened to all these poor innocent bugs?" he wondered out loud. "This is a tragic devastation, a ghastly scene," he went on, getting a little carried away. "Oh, the horror. The horror of it all."

He picked his way around the bodies gingerly.

"Pssst!" A gangly mosquito slid down the windshield toward him. *"Pssst!"* he hissed again. "Keep still, buddy!"

Barry did a double take. "What?" he said. "You're not dead?"

"Do I look dead?" the mosquito asked. "Hey, man, you'd better watch out. They'll wipe anything that moves, you know. Where are you headed, anyway?"

"To Honey Farms," Barry replied. "I'm onto something here. Something huge."

The mosquito told Barry his name was Mooseblood. "I'm on my way to Alaska."

"I'm going to Tacoma," a ladybug piped up.

"What about you?" Barry asked a fly.

The fly didn't answer.

Mooseblood cleared his throat. "He really is dead," he mumbled.

"Oh . . . OK," Barry said.

Just then a windshield wiper started to move toward them.

"See? I told you!" Mooseblood yelled. "Watch out!"

Barry's eyes went wide when he saw what was coming toward them. "What is that thing?"

"It's a wiper, dude. And . . ." The mosquito looked frightened. "And it's got triple blades!"

"Triple blades?" Barry repeated. "That doesn't sound good!"

"Jump on!" Mooseblood ordered him. "It's your only chance, bee!"

Barry followed Mooseblood's lead, leaping onto the wiper as it sliced across the glass. It swished back and forth a few times.

"Why does everything have to be so doggone clean?" Mooseblood yelled at the truck driver. "How much do you people need to see? Open your eyes! Try sticking your head out the window once in a while!"

Inside the cab of the truck, the radio was blaring. The driver and his passenger couldn't hear Mooseblood as he kept on ranting.

"Just don't kill any more bugs!" Mooseblood said. "Please stop the—"

"Oh, no," Barry whispered. He watched in horror as the mosquito was suddenly flung from the wiper.

"*Beeeeeee!*" Mooseblood shouted. "Help me!"

"Mooseblood!" Barry yelled back helplessly.

A second later, he felt himself fly off the wiper. In the nick of time, he managed to grab an antenna on the front of the truck. Nearby, a cricket on a different car was in the exact same predicament.

"*Aaaaaahhhhh!*" Barry and the cricket screamed in unison. Then another bug grabbed the antenna, screaming, too.

Inside the truck's cab, the driver looked over at his passenger. "You hear something?" he asked.

The other man shook his head. "Like what?"

"Like tiny screaming," the driver explained.

"Turn off the radio," said the passenger.

The driver reached over and pressed a button, lowering the aerial antenna that Barry had grabbed.

Barry inched up as the silver rod slowly lowered itself. Finally, only the top was still out. Barry had no choice—he had to let go.

A second later, he felt himself fly through the air. He landed inside the horn that was on top of the truck.

"Hey! What's up, bee boy?" a familiar voice said.

It was Mooseblood.

"Hey, Mooseblood!" Barry greeted him. "Good to see you!"

Barry sat down, glad to be safe. Soon he found himself telling the mosquito all about the honey display at the supermarket.

"It was just an endless row of honey jars," he said, "stretching as far as the eye could see."

"Wow." Mooseblood shook his head.

"So I'm assuming that wherever this honey truck goes, that's where they're getting it," Barry explained. "And as far as I'm concerned, that honey is ours. It belongs to the bees, not the humans."

Mooseblood nodded. "Bees hang tight."

"Well, bees are all jammed together. A hive is a close community," Barry explained.

"Not us," Mooseblood replied. "We're on our own. Every mosquito is on his own."

"But what if you get in trouble?" asked Barry. "Who's there to help you out?"

"Trouble?" Mooseblood echoed. "I've got news for you, Barry. If you're a mosquito, you're in trouble all the time. Nobody likes us. When people see a mosquito, it's *smack, smack, smack!*"

"At least you're out in the world," pointed out Barry. "You must meet a lot of girls."

"Not really." Mooseblood shook his head. "Mosquito girls usually try to trade up. They find a moth or a dragonfly or something. They don't want to be with another mosquito."

A bloodmobile had pulled up alongside the Honey Farms truck.

"Whoa!" Mooseblood said when he spotted it. "You have got to be kidding me! Mooseblood is about to leave the building!" He waved at Barry. "So long, bee."

Barry heard Mooseblood greet some other mosquitoes as he flew over to the bloodmobile.

"Hey, guys!" Mooseblood said. "I knew I'd catch you all down here! Did you bring your crazy straws?"

Barry just shook his head. He really didn't understand mosquitoes.

CHAPTER TEN

Barry fell asleep inside the horn. When he woke up later, he saw a sign along the road that said HONEY FARMS: SCHOOL GROUP TOURS AVAILABLE.

We're here, he realized with a start.

The truck came to a stop. Barry flew out of the horn and landed on the truck's hood. He pulled out his camera and snapped a few pictures of the Honey Farms sign.

Nearby, a tour guide was speaking to a group of schoolchildren. Barry saw that he wore a strange-looking hat with a wide brim, and netting that covered his face.

"All right, kids," the man told the group. "This is an apiary. It's a beehive, man-made from the cheapest wood we can find. It costs about two dollars."

He tossed aside the apiary box. It flew apart as soon as it hit the ground.

Barry zipped over to a tree and hid on it.

Fake hives! he thought. *Is that how they get the honey?*

"Hey, Freddy!" a kid yelled to the tour guide. "Why do you keep bees?"

Freddy grinned. "Because they make the honey, and we make the money!" he said.

Barry narrowed his eyes. "Just as I thought," he muttered.

"Speaking of which," Freddy went on, "it's eight dollars if you want to continue on the tour and see real-live bees."

"You already charged us four bucks just to see that box!" a kid said indignantly. "I don't have any more money!"

"Well, then," the tour guide said with a smirk. "I guess you're not going to be seeing any bees today, are you, Timmy?"

"I don't care!" Timmy declared. "I've seen bees before."

"All right then, twerp!" Freddy snapped. "Clear out of here!"

As Barry watched the scene, he could feel his dread growing.

This guy is a creep, he thought. He wondered how many bees were being held prisoner on this farm, forced to make honey for Honey Farms.

"Freddy!" another kid called. "Don't the bees sting you all the time?"

"Oh, they try," Freddy answered. He pointed to his hat. "This protects me, and then all we've got to do to stop them is give them a blast of this." He held up a strange-looking metal device with bellows attached to one end.

"What is that thing?" a boy asked, walking over.

Barry watched in horror as Freddy sent a poof of smoke right at the kids. They all started coughing.

"Hey! I don't like that thing!" a girl exclaimed.

Freddy grinned. "The bees don't like it, either. It's a smoker—and it knocks them right out!"

Barry's stinger vibrated with anger. "I'd like to knock that guy out!" he declared.

"By the time the bees wake up," Freddy went on gleefully, "the honey is ours, and they go back to the flowers."

"Hey, that rhymes!" a little boy said.

"All right, little grubbies," Freddy told the group, pointing to a fence behind them. "There are bees on the other side of that fence, if you want to see them. Otherwise, that's the end of the tour. By the way, the only way out is through the gift shop."

A kid named Bobby stood on his tiptoes, trying to peer over the fence. "I'm not tall enough to see," he complained.

"Oh, I'm sorry," Freddy said sarcastically. "Maybe I should have built an adjustable fence."

"I hate this place," Bobby grumbled.

Me, too, Barry thought.

Freddy walked away, counting all the cash he'd collected.

Barry flew after him and landed on the netting of Freddy's hat. He climbed up to the brim and peered below.

Freddy was starting to blast the apiary boxes with the smoker.

Those poor bees, Barry thought.

He hopped into an open box. Inside a tiny apartment there, two bees were barely conscious.

"Are you OK?" Barry asked.

One of the bees stood up groggily. "Yeah. We're OK. It usually doesn't last too long." He coughed a few times.

Barry looked around inside the box. "How did all these bees get here?" he asked. "Do you know you're in a fake hive? It's even got fake walls."

"I'm Howard," the bee said, introducing himself. Then he pointed to a picture of a queen bee on the wall. "Our queen was moved here; we had no choice but to follow her."

In front of them a wall slid open. Barry could see

hundreds more apiary boxes.

"What is this?" he said in horror. He pulled out his camera and began snapping pictures. "It's unbelievable. Bee honey—*our* honey—is being brazenly stolen on a massive scale."

He walked all around, snapping dozens of photos of the trapped bees and fake hives. Then he flew home as fast as he could. This was a catastrophe, a disaster for the entire bee population. Honey Farms had to be stopped, and it was up to him—Barry B. Benson—to save his species.

Back at home Barry told his parents, Uncle Carl, and his friend Adam about the scene at Honey Farms.

"This is worse than anything that bears have ever done to us," he declared. "And I intend to do something about it!"

"Oh, Barry." His mother sighed. "Please stop this."

Mr. Benson looked skeptical, too. "Son, who told you that humans are taking our honey? It's just a rumor that's been around for centuries."

Barry tossed the pictures of Honey Farms onto the table. "Do these look like rumors?" he demanded.

Uncle Carl glanced at the photos.

"Barry, the story about the humans is a conspiracy theory," he said. "These photos have obviously been doctored."

"Barry, how did you get mixed-up in all of this?" his mother wanted to know.

"He got mixed-up in it because he's been talking to humans!" Adam blurted out.

Mrs. Benson let out a gasp. *"Whaaat?"*

"You've been talking to humans?" his father echoed. "Oh, Barry. . . ."

Adam kept on going. "Not only that—he has a human girlfriend!"

Barry shot him a look. "Whose side are you on, Adam?" he demanded.

"The bees!" Adam replied.

Uncle Carl rose from his seat, pulling his pants up to his chest. "I dated a cricket once in San Antonio," he chimed in.

The others ignored him.

"Barry." Mrs. Benson looked worried. "Is this what you want to do with your life?"

"This is what I want to do for *all* of our lives," Barry said eagerly. "Nobody works harder than bees. Dad," he went on, "I remember you coming home some nights so overworked, your hands were still stirring. You couldn't stop them."

"I remember that, too," Mrs. Benson murmured.

"What right do those humans have to our hard-earned honey?" Barry said indignantly. "We're living on two cups a year. They're selling it and putting it in lip balm for no reason whatsoever. Which is why I, Barry B. Benson, intend to sue the human race," he declared. "I'm going to bring those people to their knees and deliver justice for the bees!"

CHAPTER ELEVEN

Within a few days the whole hive was buzzing about Barry's claim that humans were stealing honey from bees.

Barry's story was reported on all the local news channels, and even a famous bee TV personality wanted to interview him.

Barry sat across from the famous bee, who was named Larry, inside the TV studio.

"Tonight we're talking to Barry Benson," Larry began. He peered into Barry's face. "Did you ever think, 'I'm just a kid from the hive? I can't do this. I can't sue the entire human race'?"

Barry shook his head. "I think I've got a good case here, Larry."

Larry looked at him doubtfully. "Where I'm from, kid, you wouldn't think of suing humans. Kids concentrated on stuff like stickball and candy stores."

"How old are you?" Barry blurted out. It seemed like this guy had been on TV forever.

Larry dodged the question. "I want you to know that the entire bee community is supporting you in this case, which is certain to be the trial of the bee century."

"Thank you, Larry," Barry replied.

The TV personality turned to the camera. "Next week, it's bear week!" he declared. "They're scary, they're hairy, and they're here live!"

Barry spent the next few weeks preparing his law-suit against the humans. Vanessa was a big help; she tracked down some law books and assisted with the paperwork, too.

One night he and Adam were at the flower shop, working late. There was a knock on the front door, and Vanessa went to answer it.

"Hey, Adam," Barry called.

There was no answer.

Barry smiled when he looked over. His best friend was sound asleep inside a cinnamon-roll box.

In the other room he heard voices.

"Look, Vanessa," her tennis friend, Ken, was saying. "In tennis, you have to attack the opponent at the point of weakness."

Vanessa sounded annoyed. "Yes, Ken, but you were playing my grandmother!" she reminded him. "She's eighty-one!"

Barry did not like this guy. "Quiet, please," he said under his breath. "There's actual work going on here."

He flew over to Vanessa.

"Hey!" Ken said, spotting him. "Is that the same bee?" he asked. "The one you rescued that day?"

"Yes . . . ," Barry muttered. "It's the same bee. And what are you going to do about it?"

"I'm helping him," Vanessa told Ken. "He's suing the human race."

"What?" Ken stared at her. "You're doing what?"

Barry landed on Vanessa's shoulder.

"This is Ken, Barry," she said. "Ken, meet Barry B. Benson."

Barry didn't need an introduction. "I remember him—and his boots," he said. "Size ten and a half."

Ken blinked in surprise when he heard Barry speak. "He's talking!"

Barry puffed out his chest. "Of course I'm talking!"

Vanessa glanced back and forth between Barry and Ken. "Uh . . . Listen, Ken," she said uneasily. "I think you'd better go. We're really busy working here."

"But, Vanessa," Ken started to argue, "it's our frozen yogurt night!"

"We'll get frozen yogurt another time." She steered him toward the door. "Good night, Ken."

See ya! Barry thought, gleefully watching him exit.

♦♦♦

Barry was still hard at work when Vanessa carried coffee into the back room a little while later.

"How many sugars?" she asked.

"Just one," he told her. "I try not to use the competition," he added with a grin.

She handed him the coffee.

"Thanks," he said. They spoke softly so they wouldn't wake up Adam.

He looked at her. "So . . . why are you helping me, anyway?"

"I like you," Vanessa replied. "Bees have good qualities."

"Like what?" he asked curiously.

"Well . . ." She thought for a second. "Bees can fly, and I, myself, have never been a very good flier. Oh, and bees live all over the world, which makes them very multicultural."

Barry hopped onto the sugar cube in his coffee and rowed around like a gondolier from Italy.

"*Sì, certo!*" he replied in Italian. "It's true. Do you

ever think about"—he glanced at her shyly—"how much we have in common?"

She looked at him. "Like what?" she asked.

"Well, you like flowers, and I like flowers," he said. "And"—he gestured toward his abdomen—"I have a sweater; you have a sweater."

"OK," she said, grinning. "We do have some stuff in common."

"I have a lot of weird dreams," he went on. "Do you have a lot of weird dreams?"

"No." Vanessa shook her head. "I don't."

Barry paused. "Do you ever watch insect documentaries," he asked, "and think, hmmm, that bug is cute?"

"Not really," Vanessa admitted. She nudged him gently. "Come on. We need to get back to work."

He nodded and picked up a pen again.

You can't blame a bug for trying, he thought.

A short while later, they had finally filled out all the paperwork for the lawsuit. Together they left Vanessa's flower shop and headed out onto the street with an envelope addressed to the Superior Court.

When they reached the mailbox, Vanessa looked

On his first trip to the human world, Barry lands on a yellow flower.

"I don't think that's a flower," says one pollen jock to another.

Ouch!
Barry meets a clear glass
window for the first time.

Vanessa to the rescue!
She saves Barry from Ken.

Barry remembers his manners.
He can't leave until he
thanks Vanessa.

A talking bee!
Vanessa can't
beelieve her ears!

The beauty and the bee become good friends.

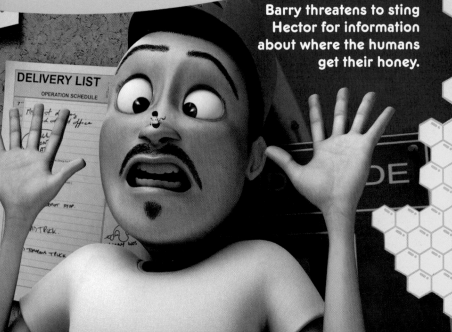

Barry threatens to sting Hector for information about where the humans get their honey.

Barry's parents just
don't understand him.
They want Barry to go
into the honey business.

On the way to Honey Farms, Barry meets a mosquito named Mooseblood.

Hive at Five: Bob Bumble reports that Barry B. Benson is suing the humans!

Vanessa helps Barry file the lawsuit.
He can't let humans steal honey
from the bees.

Cheers!
Barry toasts
their teamwork.

Barry and Vanessa win
the lawsuit with the help
of a smoking gun.

at him. "Do you realize how big this is, Barry?" she asked softly. "Are you sure—absolutely sure—that you want to go through with it?"

"Am I sure?" Barry echoed. He answered the question by kicking the fat envelope right into the mailbox. "I'm sure, all right!" he said. "When I'm done with the human race, they won't be able to say, 'Honey, I'm home!' without paying us bees!"

CHAPTER TWELVE

At last it was Barry's day in court.

In front of the courthouse, the police set up barriers to keep the crowds back. News crews camped out in front.

A newscaster stood before a TV camera.

"Brian," she said into a microphone. "It's an incredible scene here in downtown Manhattan, where for the first time, bees and humans are going to settle their differences through the court system. The bees will put aside their stingers in favor of their recently discovered verbal skills." She smiled. "I guess we'll see how persuasive they can really be."

Barry sucked in his breath as he climbed out of a cab with Vanessa and Adam.

"What have we gotten into here, Barry?" Adam asked.

"I don't know," Barry answered, taking in the mob

scene out front, "but it's pretty big, isn't it?"

They hurried past the crowd into the court-house.

Adam was amazed by all the people who'd come to watch the hearing.

Just then there was a commotion outside. Layton T. Montgomery, the defense lawyer for the humans, had arrived. As he walked toward the front doors, he deliberately squashed a bug on the pavement. Montgomery was a very large man wearing a very tiny bow tie.

Inside the courtroom, Barry felt the air grow cold.

Vanessa saw him shudder. "What's the matter?" she asked.

"I don't know . . . ," he said, his eyes fixed on Montgomery. "I just got a chill, that's all."

Montgomery strode past the table where Vanessa sat. Barry and Adam were seated at a tiny bee-sized table on top of it. Slowly, he shook a small packet of honey.

"Well, well, well," he declared loudly. "If it isn't the B-team!" He thrust the honey packet right in Barry's face. "Any of you boys work on this one?"

Just then the judge stepped into the room.

"All rise!" called out the bailiff. "The Honorable Judge Bumbleton presiding!"

The judge sat down at the bench and shuffled through some papers. "All right," she began. "Case number four thousand, four hundred and seventy-five: Superior Court of New York, *Barry B. Benson versus the Honey Industry,* is now in session." She looked at Barry. "Mr. Benson, you're representing all bees of the world, is that right?"

Barry felt his knees shake as he stood. "Yes, Your Honor."

"And Mr. Montgomery," the judge turned to the other table, "you are representing all five major food companies?"

Barry glanced over, noticing Montgomery's fancy briefcase. It had a striking emblem of an eagle that was holding a gavel in one talon and a briefcase in the other.

He shivered again.

"Yes, Your Honor," Montgomery told the judge. He puffed out his chest. "It's a privilege to represent these fine five companies."

"Your opening statement, please, then," Judge Bumbleton said.

Montgomery rose and cleared his throat. "Ladies and gentlemen of the jury," he began, "my grand-mother was a simple woman. Born on a farm, she believed it was man's divine right to benefit from the bounty of nature. If we were to live in the topsy-turvy world that Mr. Benson imagines, one in which bees own all rights to honey, just think of what it would mean." He paused dramatically and then went on. "Maybe I would have to negotiate with a silk-worm for the elastic in my britches."

A few spectators laughed.

Montgomery stared at Barry. "A talking bee!" he declared. "How do we know this isn't some sort of holographic motion-picture wizardry from Hollywood? They could be using laser beams, robotics, ventriloquism, cloning. . . . For all we know, that bee could be on steroids!"

Barry groaned inwardly. This guy would obviously say anything to get the jury on his side.

Soon it was time for Barry's opening statement.

He flew closer to the jury.

"Ladies and gentlemen," he started, "there are no illusions here, no special effects or laser beams. I'm just an ordinary bee. And as a bee," he went on, "honey is pretty important to me. It's important to all bees. We invented it, we make it, and we protect it with our lives. Unfortunately, there are some people in this room who think they can take whatever they want from us because we're the little guys. I'd like to get some of you to understand how it feels to live, work, and think like a bee. Then, I believe, you'll see, you're not only taking away our honey, you're taking away everything we *are*.

"Thank you," Barry finished.

Vanessa flashed him a thumbs-up as he went back to his seat.

"Good job, Barry," she whispered.

Barry's parents were watching at home.

"Oh, I wish he would dress like that all the time," his mother murmured. "Doesn't he look nice?"

Back in the courtroom, the two sides began calling their witnesses. Barry called the owner of Honey Farms.

"So, Mr. Klauss Vanderhayden," he said sharply. "Pretty big company you have there?"

Mr. Vanderhayden shrugged. "Yes," he said. "I suppose so."

"And I see you also own companies named Honey Burton, and Hon-Ron," Barry continued. He looked around quickly to see if Vanessa had left yet.

Good, he thought. There was no sign of her.

"Yes." Vanderhayden nodded. "Those companies provide beekeepers for our farms."

"Beekeepers?" Barry frowned. "I find that to be a very disturbing term, I have to say. I don't imagine you employ any people who are bee-*freers,* do you?"

Mr. Vanderhayden shook his head. "No," he said. "We don't."

"I'm sorry." Barry leaned in closer. "I couldn't hear you." He spelled it out slowly. "Do you employ any bee-freers—people who set bees free?"

"No," Mr. Vanderhayden said, louder this time.

"No," Barry repeated. "Because you don't free bees; you *keep* bees. And not only that"—he pointed to a jar of honey from Honey Farms—"it seems you thought a bear would be an appropriate image for a jar of honey."

"Well, bears are very lovable creatures," Mr. Vanderhayden said defensively.

"Really?" Barry snapped. "What about real bears? How do people feel about them?"

Right on cue, Vanessa reentered the courtroom.

The crowd gasped. With her was a giant, ferocious-looking grizzly bear.

Vanessa brought the bear over to where Mr. Vanderhayden sat. The bear lunged at him and let out a growl.

"Bears kill bees!" Barry reminded Vanderhayden. "How would you like his big, hairy head crashing into your living room? Biting your couch, spitting out your end tables . . ." He made a growling sound. *"Rowr, rowr!"*

The bear whirled toward Barry. *"ROWR!"*

"OK, that's enough," Barry told Vanessa quickly. "Take him away!"

Vanessa led the bear out of the courtroom.

In his seat, Mr. Vanderhayden was trembling.

Score one for the bees, Barry thought with satisfaction.

Montgomery called his next witness—the stock boy from the supermarket, Hector Hernandez.

"Mr. Hernandez," Montgomery started, "you're a stock boy at a grocery store. Have you ever had a cow come into your market and claim ownership of a quart of milk or a stick of butter?"

Hector smirked. "No," he said. Then he pointed to Barry. "But I've seen that bug a couple of times. He's a troublemaker."

"Oh, I do concur," Montgomery said smoothly. "He's quite a troublemaker."

Barry glowered at Hector.

"Next witness!" bellowed the bailiff.

CHAPTER THIRTEEN

Later that night, Barry and Vanessa sat down to eat dinner together in her apartment. The table was set with fancy dishes—including doll-sized dishes for Barry—and candles.

"This looks great," Barry said.

Vanessa glanced at her watch again. "Ken was supposed to be here," she said. "I don't know where he is. Thanks for eating with me."

Barry didn't answer. Personally, he was thrilled that Ken hadn't shown up.

While they ate, they talked about the day in court.

"The look on that woman's face, Barry!" Vanessa said. "I'm telling you, I think the jury's on our side."

"Are we doing everything right?" Barry asked her. "You know, legally?"

"I'm a florist," she reminded him, "not a lawyer. I hope we're doing everything right."

"Well, I can't believe we're actually even doing this," Barry went on. "To tell you the truth, Vanessa, I never thought I'd see you again after that first day we met."

"I never thought so, either," she said. "But I'm glad we did." She paused for a moment. "And, anyway, Barry, I think what you're doing for your species is very admirable."

"Well, they're all crazy," Barry told her. "But what are you going to do—they're my species."

She smiled. "Yes."

Barry raised his glass. "Here's to a great team."

"To a great team," Vanessa chimed in.

They clinked glasses.

Just then Ken burst into the apartment.

"Vanessa?" He froze when he saw the two of them sitting together at the dinner table. "Well, hello," he said, shooting a dark look at Barry.

"Oh ... hi, Ken!" Vanessa said, springing up. "I didn't think you were coming."

"Of course I was coming, Vanessa," he told her. "I was just running late. I tried to call you, but"—he held up a cell phone—"the battery ..."

"I didn't want all this to go to waste, so I called Barry," she explained hastily. "Luckily, he was free."

"Yeah," Barry piped up. "Luckily, I was."

Ken gritted his teeth. "Oh."

"There's still some food left," Vanessa said. "I could heat it up for you."

Ken looked away. "OK. Heat it up. Whatever."

Vanessa headed for the kitchen.

Ken sat down and glared at Barry from across the table.

"Mmmm . . ." Barry kept on eating. "This sure is delicious," he said. "It probably won't be as good when it's reheated, but she is some cook!"

"Uh-huh," was all Ken said.

"So . . . I hear you're quite a tennis player," Barry remarked.

Ken narrowed his eyes at him.

"I don't care much for the game myself," Barry said, "but . . . well . . . there you go."

"I hope I'm not interrupting anything," he went on when Ken didn't say anything.

"As a matter of fact, you are interrupting," Ken snapped. "I had something really special planned for this evening."

Barry looked at the table, where Ken was holding open a ring box. Inside was a ring—with one of those Ziamonique diamonds.

Whoa, Barry thought. *Maybe he's going to ask Vanessa to marry him.*

He watched with satisfaction as the fake-looking stone fell out of the setting.

"Oh, you know what, Ken?" Vanessa called from the kitchen. "Barry and I just rented a movie."

"What?" Ken was frantically trying to force the stone back into the ring's setting.

"You're welcome to watch with us," Vanessa went on.

"Mmmm, that'd be good," Ken answered.

Barry had finished eating. He wiped his mouth and then dropped his napkin on the table.

"I'm going to drain the old stinger," he told Ken as he headed for the bathroom.

"Yeah, you do that," Ken replied.

A few minutes later Ken stormed into the bathroom. "You think I don't see what you're doing?" he demanded.

Barry was washing his hands. "I'm sorry?" he said.

"You're trying to steal my girl!" Ken snarled. In his hands was a thick magazine.

"Whoa, dude. I'm just hanging out," Barry told him. He watched nervously as Ken began rolling up the magazine. "What's that?"

"An Italian fashion magazine," Ken told him.

Barry tried to make a joke. "*Mamma mia,* that's a lot of paper!"

Ken took a step toward Barry.

Barry eyed the magazine. "Hey! Remember what

Vanessa said? Why is your life any more valuable than mine?"

"Not to worry, bee," Ken said with a sneer. "That's exactly what I'm remembering right now!"

Ken swung the magazine at Barry. He missed, knocking everything off the vanity.

Barry zipped all around the room, trying to get away as Ken kept swinging.

Finally, Ken picked up a can of air freshener and aimed it at Barry. "Something stinks in here!" he cried, zapping him with the air freshener.

"Aaah . . . ," Barry said. "I love the smell of flowers!"

There was an evil look on Ken's face. "How do you like the smell of flames?" he snarled. With that, he pulled out a lighter, snapped it on, and lit the stream of particles from the air freshener.

"Yikes!" In a panic, Barry tried to dodge the flames. He flew around and around in a circle. Ken spun in place, desperately trying to keep up.

Suddenly, Ken's foot slipped on the thick fashion magazine. He fell backward into the shower, pulling down the shower curtain in the process. The can of air freshener hit him smack in the head, followed by the shower curtain rod and a rubber duck.

Ken reached around for another weapon. He

grabbed the handheld showerhead and held it in his hand. "Where are you, bee?" Ken growled. "I'll get you now!"

A water bug near the shower drain was nervously watching the scene.

"I'm just a water bug," he mumbled. "Just a water bug. I'm not taking sides."

Barry perched on top of the toilet tank, hiding behind a shampoo bottle. On his head he wore a helmet—the cap from a tube of lip balm.

He tried to crack a joke. "Ken, look at me!" he called. "This is pathetic!"

But Ken was still furious. He waved the showerhead in his hand. "I've got issues!" he cried, changing the setting on the nozzle from gentle to turbo, and then lethal. "There's no escape, bee!"

Ken fired the water spray at Barry, who went flying back into the toilet. All around him in the bowl were items that Ken had knocked down from the vanity—lipstick, a nail file, Q-tips.

Ken peered down into the bowl, grinning like a maniac. "Well, well, well," he declared. "Look what it is—a royal flush!"

"You're bluffing," Barry shot back. "You won't flush me."

"Oh, no?" Ken said, pushing down on the lever.

When will I learn to keep my mouth shut? Barry thought.

The water swirled around him. Desperately, Barry hopped onto the nail file—and started surfing the churning water.

As he plunged his hands into the water to steady himself, it splashed up onto Ken.

"Ewwww!" Ken screamed out. "Poo water!"

In the toilet, Barry was smoothly riding the waves. He did a few skateboard-style stunts, then surfed right out of the toilet.

He landed on the rim. "That bowl is gnarly!" he declared, grinning.

"Except for those dirty yellow rings," Ken said. He picked up the toilet brush and started swinging again.

At that moment, Vanessa stepped into the bathroom. "Kenneth!" she cried when she saw him with the toilet brush. "What are you doing?"

"You know what?" Ken replied in a strange voice. "I don't even like honey—I don't eat it!"

Vanessa looked alarmed. "We need to talk!" she told Ken. She pulled him out of the room by his ear.

Whew! Barry thought. He sat on the toilet, trying to catch his breath.

"He's just a little bee," he heard Vanessa say. "And

he happens to be the nicest bee I've met in a long time."

"A long time?" Ken echoed. "What are you talking about, Vanessa? Are there other bugs in your life?"

"No," she snapped. "But there are other things bugging me in life!"

"That's it!" Ken snarled. "I'm going out for a waffle cone!" He stomped out of the apartment.

Vanessa rushed back into the bathroom. "I'm so sorry, Barry!"

"No, please," Barry replied. "Don't be sorry. I'm actually feeling grateful right now. I was almost ex-bee-allidocious!"

Vanessa looked at him with concern. "Are you going to be OK for the trial tomorrow?" she asked.

"Sure," Barry said. "You know something, though, Vanessa?" he went on. "I don't think he likes me."

"Ken?" Vanessa asked.

"No." Barry shook his head. "The lawyer, Montgomery."

CHAPTER
FOURTEEN

The next day, Montgomery stood in front of the judge inside the crowded courtroom.

"Your Honor," he addressed her, "we would like to call Mr. Barry Benson, bee, to the stand."

As Barry took his seat, a juror wearing a striped shirt applauded.

Before Montgomery started, one of his clients waved him over.

"Layton," the businessman whispered, "you've got to weave some magic with this jury, or it's going to be all over."

"Don't worry, Mr. Gammil," Montgomery whispered back, a confident smile on his face. "I'll turn this jury around. All I have to do is remind them of what they don't like about bees.

"Do you have the tweezers?" he asked Gammil.

The client nodded, patting the pocket of his suit jacket. "Are you allergic?" he asked.

Montgomery winked at him. "Only to losing, son."

Barry waited for Montgomery to approach the stand.

"Mr. Benson," Montgomery began. "I'll ask you what I think we'd all like to know. What exactly is your relationship to"—he whirled and pointed a finger at Vanessa—"that woman?"

"We're friends," Barry said calmly.

"Good friends?" Montgomery asked.

"Yes," Barry replied.

Montgomery swiftly changed the subject. "I've seen a bee documentary or two," he said. "Now, from what I understand, your queen gives birth to *all* the bee children in the hive?"

"Yes, but—" Barry tried to argue.

Montgomery spun toward where Barry's parents sat. "So those aren't even your real parents!"

"Oh, Barry," Mr. Benson murmured.

"Yes, they are!" Barry shouted.

Adam couldn't stand watching Montgomery for one more minute. He flew up from his seat. "Hold me back!" he shouted. "This guy is a monster!"

Vanessa held him down with a coffee stirrer.

By now, all the bees in the courtroom were humming with anger.

"He's denouncing bees!" Adam shouted.

Montgomery licked his lips. "So I guess that means

you all date your own cousins," he said to Barry.

Vanessa jumped to her feet, letting go of Adam. "Objection, Your Honor, objection!" she shouted.

Adam exploded into the air, headed right for Montgomery. "I'm going to pincushion this guy!" he yelled.

"Adam, don't!" Barry warned him. "It's what he wants!"

Montgomery grinned when he saw Adam zooming toward him. Deliberately, he turned around and stuck out his rear end, giving Adam a wide-open target.

Barry tried to block Adam's path. But Adam shoved Barry out of the way. Then he shot forward and stung Montgomery right in the butt.

The jury gasped.

"*Ow!*" Montgomery howled. "I'm hit! I'm hit!"

The judge banged her gavel hard. "Order! Order!" she shouted.

Montgomery was still moaning and rolling around on the floor.

"Please, Mr. Montgomery," the judge warned him. "Don't put on a big show for everyone."

But there was no stopping the lawyer's theatrics.

"The venom!" Montgomery wailed. "The venom is coursing through my veins! I have been felled by a winged beast of destruction!" He looked toward the jury to make sure they were watching. "You see? You can't treat bees like equals. They're savages—striped savages! And stinging is the only thing they know! It's their way!"

Barry had rushed over to Adam's side. "Adam . . . ," he murmured. "Stay with me. Stay with me, buddy."

Adam moaned. "Barry, I can't feel my legs."

Barry's heart sank. Adam needed help fast, or—

Montgomery fell on the bailiff, continuing his rant against bees.

The judge frantically banged her gavel again. "Please, I will have order in this court. Order! Order, please!"

That evening everyone in the hive was talking about the dramatic events in court. On TV, a newscaster summed it up grimly.

"The case of the honeybees versus the human race took a pointed turn against the bees today when one member of their legal team stung Layton T. Montgomery. . . ."

Barry knew things did not look good for his side. All he could think about, however, was his best buddy, Adam. He hurried to the hospital.

Adam lay in bed with the TV on.

"Hey, buddy," Barry said.

"Hey," Adam replied softly.

"Is there much pain?" Barry asked.

There was a button near Adam's head that controlled the amount of pain medication he got. "Yeah . . . ," Adam replied, pressing the button. "It hurts a lot." Then he looked at Barry. "I blew the whole case, didn't I?"

"It doesn't matter," Barry reassured him. "The most important thing is you're alive. You could have died."

"I'd be better off dead," Adam muttered. "Look at me!"

He threw off the blanket, showing Barry his fake stinger. It was a green toothpick sword with a handle at the top.

"They got it from the cafeteria," Adam explained bitterly. "It was in a tuna sandwich. Look. There's still a little celery on it." He showed Barry.

Barry didn't know what to say. "What was it like to sting someone?" he asked finally.

Adam looked away for a second. "I can't explain it," he replied. "It was all adrenaline . . . and then . . . ecstasy."

Barry nodded. He couldn't really imagine the feeling.

"Do you think it was a trap?" Adam wanted to know. "Did Montgomery try to get us mad on purpose?"

"Of course," Barry replied. "I'm sorry, Adam. I

flew us right into this. What were we thinking? Look at us—we're just a couple of bugs in this world."

"What do you think the humans will do to us if they win?" Adam asked.

"I don't know," Barry admitted. "Look at their history with other insects—ant farms, flea circuses, roach motels. They're obviously capable of anything."

"Oh, my." Adam sighed.

The window near Adam's bed was open, and Barry could hear people talking outside on the sidewalk below. They were obviously smoking, too, because a cloud of smoke rose into the air and drifted into the room.

Adam coughed a few times. "Barry? Could you do me a favor and get a nurse to close that window?"

"Why?" asked Barry.

"The smoke," Adam explained. "Bees don't smoke."

"Right . . . ," Barry said. "Bees don't smoke." As he started for the nurse's station down the hall, something occurred to him.

He whirled around and rushed back to Adam's room.

"But some bees are smoking, Adam! That's it!" he cried. "I've just figured out how to win our case!"

CHAPTER FIFTEEN

The next session in court came a few days later. Adam was out of the hospital by then.

He sat at the table, nervously watching for Barry and Vanessa to appear.

Montgomery wore a neck brace and rolled into the room in an electric wheelchair, acting as if he'd been gravely wounded by the sting from Adam.

The judge tapped her fingers on the desk. "Mr. Flayman," she addressed Adam.

"Yes?" He cast another look at the door. "Yes, Your Honor?" he said.

"Where is the rest of your team?" she demanded. "We cannot wait all day."

Adam fumbled with his artificial stinger. "Well, Your Honor," he began, "it's sort of an interesting story. You know that bees are trained to fly haphazardly, and as a result, we sometimes don't make very good time. I actually once heard a pretty funny story about a bee—"

Montgomery cut him off. "Your Honor," he said impatiently. "Haven't these ridiculous bugs taken up enough of this court's valuable time?"

Montgomery rolled out from behind his table.

"How much longer are we going to allow these absurd shenanigans to go on?" Montgomery demanded. "The bees have presented no compelling evidence to support their charges. My clients all run perfectly legitimate businesses," Montgomery added. "I move for a complete dismissal of the entire case."

The judge looked at Adam. "Mr. Flayman, I'm afraid I am going to have to consider Mr. Montgomery's motion."

"But you can't!" Adam pleaded. "We have a terrific case against these guys!"

"Where is your proof?" Montgomery demanded. "Where is the evidence? Show me the smoking gun!"

At that moment, Barry burst through the door. "Hold it, Your Honor!" he yelled.

Right behind him was Vanessa, carrying a bee smoker.

Barry had heard Montgomery's last remark. "You want a smoking gun?" he demanded. "Here's your smoking gun!"

Vanessa slammed the beekeeper's smoker onto the judge's bench.

"What is that thing?" the judge demanded.

The bee smoker billowed puffs of white smoke.

"What, this thing?" Montgomery grabbed it. "This harmless contraption couldn't hurt a fly—let alone a bee."

Without thinking, Montgomery swung it toward the side of the courtroom where the bees were sitting. Instantly, they were all knocked out.

The jury gasped in horror. Members of the press jumped to their feet and started snapping pictures of the unconscious bees.

It was Barry's turn to make a dramatic statement.

"Members of the jury," he began, "look at what has happened to innocent bees, who have never been asked, 'Smoking or non?' Is this what nature intended for us?"

Montgomery's clients suddenly looked very nervous.

"What are we going to do?" Gammil whispered.

"He's playing the species card," Montgomery murmured. "Don't worry. It won't work."

"I implore you," Barry went on. "I appeal to your humanity. . . ." He flew over to the scale of justice near the judge's bench. It balanced as he landed. Then he zipped across the room to the railing so he could speak directly to the jury.

"Please do the right thing, ladies and gentlemen," he pleaded. "Please, free the bees!"

"Free the bees!" the jury started chanting. "Free the bees! Free the bees!"

The judge pounded her gavel, and then announced her decision. "The court finds in favor of the bees!"

Inside the courtroom, total chaos erupted.

Barry flew over to Vanessa. "We won, Vanessa!" he cried. "We won!"

"Yay!" she cheered. "I knew you could do it!"

She high-fived Barry, sending him crashing to the table.

"Ooops!" she apologized. "Sorry about that."

"I'm OK," Barry told her. "Vanessa, do you realize what this means?" he went on. "Now bees will be the only ones who can own honey. Those jars and packets—they're finally all ours!"

Montgomery stomped past them, wagging a finger at Barry. "This will completely upset the balance of nature, Benson! You'll regret this!"

"With all due respect, sir," Barry shot back, "the balance of nature is how we make our living!"

Montgomery opened the door to the courtroom. Media people poured in, making a beeline for Barry.

"Barry! Barry! Mr. Benson!" they clamored, crowding around him. "Can we get a statement?"

"All right, all right," he replied. "One at a time."

Adam and Vanessa stood back, gathering up their team's paperwork.

"We should go celebrate," Vanessa said.

"Right ...," Adam said absentmindedly. He wanted to celebrate their victory, but something was gnawing at him.

"What if Montgomery's right?" he asked suddenly.

Vanessa looked at him. "What do you mean?" she asked.

"We've been living the bee way for a long time," Adam replied. "Twenty-seven million years. Maybe Montgomery had a point about upsetting the balance of nature."

Barry could barely make it outside the courthouse. Reporters were still thronging him, asking him questions about the case.

"Congratulations on your victory," a newscaster called. "What are you going to demand as a settlement? You could get billions from these companies."

Barry shook his head. "This was never about money," he said. "We bees only want what was ours to begin with."

"So what are you going to ask for?" another guy yelled.

"We're going to demand a complete shutdown of all human-led honey production," Barry told them. "Our honey does not belong in lozenges, hams, or buffalo wings. . . . And we will confiscate all illegal honey in the hands of nonbees by any means necessary.

"And not only that," Barry went on, "we demand an end to the glorification of the bear as anything more than a filthy, smelly, big-headed, bad-breath stink machine!" He lowered his voice. "I believe we're all aware of what they do in the woods. And finally, we will no longer tolerate derogatory names for bees. A new day has dawned, ladies and gentlemen!"

All around him bees cheered again.

Like Barry, they had no idea about the dark days that lay ahead.

CHAPTER SIXTEEN

Twenty-four hours later, the gates to Honey Farms and other honey companies were locked forever. Government agents from the new ATFH Bureau (Alcohol, Tobacco, Firearms, and Honey) began policing restaurants, stores, and people's homes, enforcing the new law that made it illegal for humans to eat or use any products that contained honey.

At Honex Industries, the bees had never produced so much honey. Shortly after the humans stopped using honey, the level in the storage tank shot up to the three-cup mark.

A worker flew up to see Buzzwell.

"Sir, we just passed three cups," he told him in a panic, "and there are more gallons coming! We don't have room to store it all!"

Buzzwell was trying to keep his cool. "I am aware

of the situation," he told the worker. Then he made an emergency announcement over the loudspeaker. "Cease all honey production! Cease all honey production at once!"

The whistle blew and all the bees quickly exited the building.

With all that honey, there was no need for the bees to make more. Soon even the pollen jocks had stopped working. There were no bees out collecting nectar from flowers, and thus no bees spreading pollen around from plant to plant.

As the days passed, grass and other plants began to turn brown. Flowers wilted and then died.

Vanessa's business was hit hard. She was forced to hang a sign on the door of her shop that said: CLOSED UNTIL FURTHER NOTICE. SORRY.

At first, Barry didn't realize what was happening.

One day he flew to Honex Industries, eager to talk to Adam about all the honey he had collected from the humans.

Barry landed in Adam's office. Papers were strewn about everywhere, and Adam was packing up boxes.

"Adam!" Barry exclaimed. "You wouldn't believe how much honey people were using—they were putting it in everything—soap, candles, nuts. Now it's all ours again."

"Really?" Adam said in a flat tone. "That's great."

Barry looked around, suddenly noticing the empty corridors. "Hey, what's going on around here?" he asked. "Where is everybody?"

Adam started out the door carrying a cardboard box of his things. "I don't know." He shrugged. "They're at the beach, in their pools. I heard that your uncle Carl is on his way to San Antonio with a cricket."

"I don't get it." Barry followed him along the empty hallway, still perplexed.

Adam motioned toward a bunch of coats on hooks. "The workers left so fast, they didn't even take their coats."

"Wow," Barry murmured. "That's incredible."

Adam turned to look at him. "We had a unique purpose, Barry. And so what if we weren't the only ones who liked honey?" he went on. "We were still the only ones who could make it."

"But now we don't need to make it all the time," Barry argued. "We can take time off, relax a little."

"You're right," Adam said with a sigh. "We don't need to do anything. See you later, Barry."

Frowning, Barry watched him go. For the first time since he'd won his court case against the humans, he felt something settle deep in the pit of his stomach.

It was worry.

Later that day, Barry followed Vanessa to the roof of her apartment building so that she could show him something.

"Nobody's working," he told her. "Honex is deserted. Everybody's just at home, doing nothing."

"Hmmm . . . ," Vanessa murmured.

"It's terrible," Barry went on. "I wanted everyone in my hive to have a better life. But I guess it's true—honey changes people."

"Barry." Vanessa stopped for a second. "You don't have any idea what's going on, do you?"

He looked at her uneasily. "What did you want to show me?" he asked.

"This," Vanessa replied. They reached the top of the stairs and Vanessa opened the door.

Barry gaped. On the rooftop, all of the plants Vanessa had been growing were brown.

"What happened here?" Barry asked.

"This isn't the half of it," she said gravely.

She spun him around so that he could look out over the city at the park. The grass—along with all the trees and shrubs and flowers—had turned completely brown.

"Oh, no!" Barry burst out. "Everything is dying."

"It doesn't look very good, does it?" Vanessa replied.

He shook his head.

"And whose fault do you think this is?" she asked him.

"You know, I'm going to guess," he answered. "I think it's maybe the bees' fault."

"The bees' fault?" Vanessa echoed.

"Well, specifically this bee—me," Barry said. "I guess I wasn't thinking. It never occurred to me that if the bees stopped making honey, everything would be affected."

"It's not just plants and flowers," Vanessa told him. "It's fruits, vegetables—they all need bees to grow.

"And," she went on, "when you take away what animals eat, it affects the entire animal kingdom. And then, of course it affects—"

"Humans," he jumped in. "Humans need plants, too."

"Yes." She cleared her throat. "We do."

"So what you're saying is," Barry continued, "if there's no more pollination, everything on the planet could die."

He looked away, upset.

"This is partly my fault," Vanessa said softly. "I helped you free the bees."

Barry let out a long sigh. "Why didn't I just become a stirrer like everybody wanted me to do?"

"Barry, listen," Vanessa said. "I'm sorry, but I've got to get going."

Without another word, she turned around and hurried down the stairs.

"Vanessa!" he cried. He flew after her as she rushed out to the street and hailed a cab.

"Vanessa! Why are you leaving?" he asked. "Where are you going?"

A cab stopped for her, and Barry followed her into the backseat.

"I'm going to the Tournament of Roses Parade in Pasadena," she told him sadly. "They had to move it up to this weekend because all the flowers are dying. You know how I've always wanted to go," she went on. "It's the last chance I'll ever have to see it."

"Vanessa . . ." Barry felt terrible. "I just want to say, I'm so sorry. I never meant for things to turn out like this."

She gave him a small smile. "I know. Me neither."

"I'll see you when you get back," he mumbled. "Bye."

Barry hovered in front of the Vanessa's flower shop. "I wish someone would swat me right now," he said miserably. "I've ruined everything—the trees, the flowers, Vanessa's business. . . ."

His eyes landed on the poster for the Tournament of Roses.

"Roses . . . ," he murmured. "Wait a minute—roses! Roses!" he shouted. "Vanessa!" he yelled.

He zoomed down the street after her cab. "Vanessa!" he cried, pounding on the window. "Vanessa!"

She rolled down the window.

"Roses!" he said.

"Barry?" she said uncertainly.

He flew alongside the cab. "Roses are flowers," he told her.

"Yes, they are," she answered, totally confused.

"Flowers, bees, pollen!" Barry burst out, as if that explained everything.

"I know, Barry," she said patiently. "That's why this is the last parade. I'm sorry to say that soon there won't be any more flowers."

"Maybe not," he said. "But I have an idea."

By now the cab was speeding ahead of him. Barry asked Vanessa to tell the driver to slow down.

Then he flew inside with her. "Vanessa, listen," he

said. "I think I've figured out a way to fix all this."

"What can you do?" she asked.

"Well, if they have roses at the parade," he began, "the roses will have pollen, right? And if we could somehow get that pollen and bring it back—that's all we need!"

She blinked. "Are you saying we can repollinate the park?"

"It's a start," he informed her.

"So that's your plan?" she asked.

"Yes," he said, beaming. "It's plan B!"

CHAPTER SEVENTEEN

Barry looked around in awe as he and Vanessa approached the security gate. Outside the float staging area, people bustled all around them. Beyond the gate were massive motorized floats decorated with all kinds of flowers—roses, gardenias, tulips, carnations—and many others that he didn't even recognize.

He turned to Vanessa. "We made it to the Tournament of Roses!" he declared. "But these are the last flowers on earth. I bet everything will be locked down tight."

"I can handle the security," Vanessa told him. "Watch this."

Barry pretended to be a brooch pinned to Vanessa's shirt.

A heavily armed guard stood in front of the gate, blocking Vanessa's way. "No one goes beyond this point except for authorized personnel," he told her.

She held out a hand. "Vanessa Bloome, on official floral business," she said.

"Oh, sorry," the guard instantly apologized, then swung open the gate. "Come on in, Miss Bloome. That's a nice brooch."

"Thank you. It was a gift," she said as she walked past.

Inside, there was even more activity. A line of floats had begun moving slowly along the parade route. People stood on each side of the street, waving and applauding as the elaborate floats streamed past.

Barry repeated the plan to Vanessa. "Once we spot a vulnerable-looking float, we can jump aboard and—"

"There's one," Vanessa interrupted. She pointed to a huge float that was decorated to look like a scene from the fairy tale The Princess and the Pea. "I think we might be able to commandeer that one, Barry."

He nodded, eyeing the princess who was sitting alone on top of a pile of mattresses, already waving to the crowd.

"All we need to do is replace the princess," he said.

In an instant they were ready. Barry wrapped himself in a green leaf so he'd look like a pea. Then he flew up to distract the princess while Vanessa went around to the side of the float to remove the ladder.

"Sorry I'm late, Princess," he called. "Where should I sit?"

The princess looked at him, confused. "What?" she said. "Who are you?"

"I believe I'm the pea," he answered.

"The pea?" she echoed. "There's no pea on this float! It's supposed to be *under* all the mattresses—not on top of them."

"Not in this version of the fairy tale, sweetheart!" he informed her.

"This is ridiculous!" The princess stood up in huff. "I'm going to talk to the parade marshal," she declared.

"You do that," Barry replied. "This whole parade is a fiasco anyway!"

She stalked off toward the ladder to exit. "I can't believe this. I—"

Barry heard a shout of surprise as she tumbled off the float.

Good work, Vanessa! he thought.

Two minutes later, Vanessa was beside Barry, wearing the woman's princess hat.

"All we have to do now is drive the float out of

the parade without arousing suspicion," Barry told her. He quickly hot-wired it so they could drive away when they were ready.

The floats were moving slowly along the parade route. People *ooh*ed and *aah*ed at the colorful flowers and elaborate decorations as they passed.

Barry gave Vanessa the signal, and suddenly she accelerated. Their float lurched forward, flying past the crowds and crashing through a tall fence. Vanessa steered the float onto the freeway.

"We did it!" she called. "This thing handles pretty well!"

Barry breathed in the flowers' sweet scent. "The smell is fantastic!" he said.

"We only have about twenty minutes to catch the next plane home," Vanessa reminded him.

They sped along the highway toward the airport.

"All we have to do now is figure out a way to get this float on a flight," Barry said.

"Piece of cake!" Vanessa called back.

At the airport they pulled up to the curb.

An airport worker wearing a red cap walked over.

"May I help you with your luggage?" he asked.

"Oh, yes," Vanessa replied, stalling while Barry tried to figure out a way to deal with the huge float.

"I'm a real princess," Vanessa went on. "I'm from the kingdom of . . . Bensonia!"

"What?" The guy with the red cap blinked at her. "You're a princess?"

"Oh, yes," she said. "And back in Bensonia, we . . ." She blabbered on, telling him all about her kingdom. "And we need to check this float," she concluded.

Barry slapped a luggage tag onto the float.

"Come on, Vanessa," he said. "We've got a plane to catch!"

Barry and Vanessa raced through the airport, making their flight in the nick of time.

As the plane took off, Barry let out a sigh of relief. "That was close, but we pulled it off," he said. "And if we're very lucky, we'll have enough pollen to do the job."

He hopped onto Vanessa's laptop computer and did some complicated calculations involving numbers of bees, flowers, and pollen, along with the plane's airspeed.

At last he did a little happy dance on the keyboard. "Guess what, Vanessa? We're very lucky. We have just enough pollen to get this done!"

"It's got to work, Barry," she replied. "Or else—"

"Attention, passengers!" Just then the pilot's voice came over the loudspeaker. "This is Captain Scott! I'm afraid we have a bit of bad weather in the New York area," he announced. "It looks like we're going to be experiencing a delay."

"Uh-oh." Vanessa turned to Barry. "We have cut flowers on board with no water," she said in a worried tone. "They're never going to survive a longer trip."

Barry nodded. "I've got to get up there and talk to these guys," he said.

"Be careful," Vanessa called after him.

Barry shot up front and knocked on the door of the cockpit.

"Hey!" he called. "I believe I ordered a kosher meal!"

A flight attendant was in the cockpit chatting with the pilots. She rolled her eyes when she heard Barry complaining.

"Excuse me," she said in an irritated voice. "I'd better go deal with this guy."

Barry was hiding on the yellow-and-black emergency stripe when she opened the door.

It was the perfect camouflage. The flight attendant looked around, but didn't see anyone. Barry zipped right into the cockpit before the door closed. The bee was alone with the pilots.

"Excuse me, Captain," he said. "I am in a real situation here."

Captain Scott pulled an earphone off his ear and looked at the copilot next to him. "What did you say, Hal?"

"I didn't say anything," the copilot replied.

Barry hovered in front of the captain.

"*Aaah!*" the pilot cried. "A bee!"

"No, no!" Barry said in a rush. "Don't freak out. Please don't freak out! There's a chance that my entire species will—"

The copilot slipped off his earphones, too. When he spotted Barry, he let out a yelp.

Then he grabbed a small handheld vacuum cleaner and aimed it at Barry, trying to suck him up.

Barry danced away from the vacuum cleaner. "No," he cried. "You've got to listen to me! Please!"

As the copilot chased Barry all around the cockpit, the toupee on the man's head slid off. It landed near the vacuum cleaner and instantly got sucked into the machine.

Barry jumped onto the bald man's head.

"Wait a minute!" he called, desperately. "Please listen to me. I'm an attorney!"

The copilot looked around, trying to figure out where the voice was coming from. "Who's an attorney?" he demanded. "Who's saying that?"

"Don't move!" Captain Scott suddenly commanded.

The copilot froze as Captain Scott tiptoed over to him with the vacuum.

"I've got him now!" Captain Scott declared.

He swung the vacuum at the copilot's head, trying to mash Barry. But Barry reacted fast. He dropped down, hovering in front of the copilot's nose. The vacuum struck the copilot hard, knocking him out. He fell backward onto a button marked LIFE RAFT RELEASE.

"Oh, no," Barry groaned as the life raft burst open and instantly filled with air. It slammed Captain Scott into a wall, knocking him out cold.

Barry gazed around the cockpit in dismay.

"Oh, Barry," he scolded himself. "What have you done now?"

CHAPTER EIGHTEEN

On the plane's cabin, Vanessa was typing on her laptop when a voice came over the PA system. "Good afternoon, passengers, this is your captain speaking."

Vanessa looked up in surprise. That wasn't the captain speaking, she realized. It was Barry!

"Would a Miss Vanessa Bloome in seat forty-two D please report to the cockpit?" Barry went on in his official captain voice. "And please hurry, Miss Bloome!"

Vanessa undid her seat belt and raced up the aisle. Her heart pounded as she rushed into the cockpit.

"Oh, no . . . ," she murmured when she saw the two pilots lying there unconscious. "What happened here, Barry?" she asked.

He had no idea how to explain it to her. "I tried to

talk to them," he began, "but there was a vacuum and a toupee . . . and then the life raft exploded . . . and now one's bald and they're both unconscious. . . ."

Vanessa blinked at him. "Is that another bee joke?" she demanded. "I have no idea what you're talking about."

He shook his head. "Unfortunately, it's no joke," he said grimly. "And now no one is flying the plane."

The radio crackled.

"This is your airport control tower," an air traffic controller said. "Flight three five six, what is your status?"

Vanessa spoke into the intercom. "This is Vanessa Bloome. I'm a florist from New York."

"This is Bud Ditchwater," the air traffic controller replied. "Miss Bloome, where is the pilot?"

"He's"—Vanessa cleared her throat—"he's . . . er . . . unconscious," she said finally. "And so is the copilot."

"Not good," Bud replied. "Is there anyone onboard who has flight experience?"

There was a long pause as Barry and Vanessa exchanged looks.

"As a matter of fact," Barry answered, "there is."

"Who's that?" asked Bud.

"Barry Benson," Vanessa told him.

"That bee from the honey trial?" Bud groaned loudly. "Oh, great."

Vanessa was looking at Barry doubtfully, too.

"I can handle it," Barry tried to reassure her. "I've been flying for my entire life. This plane is nothing more than a big metal bee," he went on. "It's just got giant wings and huge engines."

"Stay on course and we'll get right back to you," Bud told them. "Over and out."

"Barry . . ." Vanessa was worried. "What are we going to do?"

"We're going to land this plane," Barry said firmly. "You know how important flowers are?"

"Of course," she replied. "I'm a florist."

"Well, there you go," he said. "Now I'll just do what I would do, and you use the flight controls to make the wings of the plane copy me, OK?"

"OK," she agreed, but her voice was filled with doubt.

Back in New Hive City, the Benson family was watching TV with Adam when an announcer suddenly interrupted the show.

"This is Bob Bumble," the newscaster said. "We have some late-breaking news from the airport, where a very suspenseful scene is developing. Barry Benson, fresh off his stunning legal victory over honey corporations, is—"

Adam sprang up from the couch. "That's Barry!" he declared.

"That's right, folks," Bob Bumble repeated, "he's attempting to land a plane. It's loaded with people, flowers, and an incapacitated flight crew."

"Flowers?" The bees in the Bensons' living room echoed. "The plane is carrying flowers?"

"Oh, my goodness," Mrs. Benson murmured.

They sat there, glued to the TV set.

"All right, pull back," Barry ordered Vanessa. "See how my head's coming up here a little?"

Vanessa watched Barry, then frantically tried to imitate his movements with the plane's wings.

"OK ... OK ...," she said. "Uh-oh. Wait a minute, Barry." An alarmed expression crossed her face as she read the radar screen. "We're headed straight into a storm!"

"We have no choice, Vanessa," Barry said quickly. "Think of the flowers. If we don't get to New York soon, they'll die. There's no time to fly around the storm."

Outside, dark clouds surrounded the plane. Lightning flashed ominously.

Vanessa gripped the controls as the plane cut through the storm.

In the Air Traffic Control tower, people and bees from the media surrounded Bud, desperate to know what was going on. Like Barry and Vanessa, Bud was trying not to panic.

"Well, we have a massive storm front moving into the area," he announced solemnly. "And two individuals at the controls of a jumbo jet with absolutely no flight experience."

"Just a minute, Mr. Ditchwater," the bee newscaster, Jeanette Chung, piped up. "I'm not sure they have no flight experience—there's a honeybee on that plane."

"Oh, I'm quite familiar with Mr. Benson's work—and his no-account friends," Bud shot back. "Haven't they done enough damage already? Thanks to them, there are no flowers anymore. My daughter had to wear a bundle of twigs on her wrist to her prom. It caught fire while she was dancing to that crazy music!"

"At least he has flight experience," Jeanette Chung reminded Bud. "So, isn't he your only hope for saving that plane right now?"

"A honeybee?" Bud scoffed. "Come on, technically a bee shouldn't be able to fly at all. With their shape, they violate virtually every law of aviation known to man!"

Aboard the plane, Barry could hear every word that Bud was saying.

"Their wings are too small," Bud went on, "their bodies are too big, and I'm not crazy about those stripes, either!"

Barry had heard enough. "Hey! Hold on a second! Haven't we heard this a million times already?" he said. "The surface area of our wings and our body mass doesn't add up. Based on the numbers, we shouldn't be able to fly."

"Get this on the air!" Jeanette Chung commanded her news crew. "Now!"

"You got it!" a cameraman answered, springing into action.

In the Bee TV control room, an engineer threw a switch.

"Stand by," the engineers said. "We're going live."

An ON AIR sign lit up.

The news story about Barry and the air controller's comments played on TVs everywhere in New Hive City. Buzzwell from Honex saw the report. So did the pollen jocks and the hundreds of bees hanging out in the street.

"As bees, our lives are based on doing things that people say we can't do," Barry was saying. "That's why I want to get the bees back to doing what makes us bees—working together."

Everywhere bees stood still, riveted to their TVs.

"It's the bee way," Barry said. "We get behind a fellow. Black and yellow!"

Bees cheered loudly.

Meanwhile, Barry had a job to do.

"How are we doing on time?" he asked Vanessa.

"Not great," she admitted. "The gardenias are very delicate. They could be starting to lose it."

"Oh, no," Barry said. "This is not good, not good at all."

CHAPTER NINETEEN

Back in New Hive City, the pollen jocks had moved into action. Lou Duva met them at the J-Gate.

"All of you!" he commanded. "Let's move it out!"

Thousands of other bees began flying to the airport.

Aboard the plane, Barry continued calling out instructions to Vanessa. "Left, right, down, hover," he said.

She gave him a look. "Hover?"

"Forget hover," he replied.

A fierce bolt of lightning suddenly shot through the sky. It struck the plane, shorting out the radio.

"Barry!" Vanessa cried in a panic. "We've lost contact with the tower!"

On the ground, the team of air controllers looked at each other.

"We've lost contact," one murmured. "This is definitely not good."

Barry was sure things couldn't get much worse. Then an alarm sounded inside the cockpit of the plane.

"Oh, no!" Vanessa cried. "Barry, we have to land soon, or we'll be out of fuel!"

"How much fuel is left?" he asked, afraid to know the answer.

They both heard an engine turbine wind down—and then stop.

"I'm guessing none," Vanessa said in a small voice.

The other engine turbine stopped.

"Oh, no. What's going to happen to us?" Vanessa asked, choking back tears.

The plane started to drop. Barry's insides lurched as they plummeted through the dark sky. Vanessa screamed in terror.

This is it, he thought in despair. *After all this work, we'll never—*

And then, to his astonishment, he felt something lurch under the plane. The plane stabilized, and then its nose suddenly lifted back up toward the sky.

"Barry!" Vanessa cried. "What's going on?"

His antennae vibrated before he could reply.

"Hello?" he answered the phone.

"Hey, Benson!" a familiar voice greeted him. It was Lou Duva. "Have you got any flowers in there for a happy occasion?"

Relief washed over Barry.

"We're saved!" he told Vanessa. "It's the pollen jocks!"

Lou, Buzz, Splitz, and Jackson flew up alongside the cockpit.

"Wow!" Vanessa was amazed. "They really do get behind a fellow," she said.

Barry grinned. "Black and yellow," he declared.

"All right, you two!" Lou Duva said into Barry's headset. "What do you say we drop this tin can on the blacktop?"

"Blacktop?" Vanessa repeated, looking through the windshield. "What blacktop? I can't see anything. Can you?"

Barry shook his head. "Not a thing. It's all gray," he answered.

In the Air Traffic Control room, the crew was deeply worried.

"I don't know how they're going to do it," Bud said. "With this weather, even an experienced pilot would have trouble seeing the runway."

A few others murmured their agreement.

"Nearly impossible," one remarked.

Adam was with the other bees along the runway. He knew that Barry couldn't hear him, but he was coaching him all the same.

"Come on, Barry," Adam said. "You've got to think bee. Thinking bee, thinking bee."

Together the swarm of bees formed a gigantic flower on the runway. As they moved together, the flower flashed two colors, black and yellow.

Soon they had all picked up Adam's chant.

Thinking bee . . . thinking bee . . . thinking bee. . . .

Up in the plane all Barry could see through the windshield was a swirl of mist and clouds.

"I still can't see anything," he told Vanessa. But then inside his belly, an odd sensation rippled through him.

"Wait a minute . . . ," he murmured. "I think I'm feeling something."

Vanessa looked at him. "What do you mean, Barry?"

"I don't know," Barry told her. "But it's strong. And it's pulling me . . . like . . . like . . . a twenty-seven-million-year-old instinct."

"Huh?" Vanessa said, confused. "It's pulling you to what?"

"Bring the nose down!" he commanded suddenly. Then he used his antennae to send out an order to the pollen jocks. "Guys, cut your power by fifty percent!"

Lou Duva picked up the order. "Cut power fifty percent!" he called to his troops.

Below on the runway, the bees were still chanting, *"Thinking bee . . . thinking bee. . . ."*

An air traffic controller jumped to his feet inside the tower. "What in the world is on the tarmac?" he cried.

They all rushed to the window to look below.

It was the bees' gigantic flower.

"Get some lights on that!" shouted Bud.

Within minutes, lights were rolled onto the side of the runway, lighting up the bees' flower formation.

Barry spotted it, too.

"Vanessa! Aim for the flower!" he told her. "Ready, boys?" he said to the pollen jocks. "Give me full reverse. Vanessa, flaps down!"

Vanessa followed his instructions, aiming the plane down toward the flower.

In the plane's cargo hold, the float from the rose parade bumped into the door's release button. Millions of flowers spilled out below, onto the runway.

Barry carefully guided Vanessa as she worked the controls.

"Good, good, easy now," he said. "That's it. Easy, just let it down. Full forward."

"We're coming in too fast!" Vanessa cried.

Barry reported this to Lou Duva.

"Ready, boys?" he said. "Give me full reverse. Full reverse, nose down. Bring your tail up. Rotate around it."

"This is insane, Barry," Vanessa said. "We're moving in a crazy pattern. We're not bugs—we're flying a plane!" she reminded him.

He tried to stay calm. "This is the only way I know how to fly," he said. "I have to do it my way."

Bud watched the plane in disbelief. "Am I cuckoo, or is that plane flying in an insectlike pattern?" he asked his coworkers.

They were all too busy watching to answer.

"Get your nose in there," Barry told Vanessa. "Don't be afraid. Smell it. Full reverse! Easy, just drop it. Be a part of it. Aim for the center! Now drop it in. Drop it in, woman!"

The plane hovered close to the ground for a moment and then maneuvered its way into the center of the giant flower—exactly like a bee!

Inside the plane's cabin, the passengers sat frozen for a minute.

Then the inflatable slides popped out the side of the plane, and they rushed over to exit. In the cockpit, Vanessa and Barry did the same thing.

They stood together on the tarmac.

Vanessa let out a deep breath. "Barry, we did it!" she exclaimed. "You taught me how to fly!"

"Plus, we saved the flowers," Barry reminded her. "And the people. And the pollen."

"And you saved my life," Vanessa added.

"High five!" he said. They slapped hands together. Adam hurried over to his friends.

"Barry!" he cried. "It worked! Did you see our giant flower?"

"Of course I saw the flower!" Barry told him. "That was genius, man, genius!"

"Thank you," Adam replied modestly.

"There's just one more thing," Barry said. He zipped up to the wing and cupped his hands so he could make an announcement to the swarm of bees.

"Listen, everyone!" he called. "Our job isn't done yet. This runway is covered with the last pollen from the last flowers available anywhere on earth. That means this is our last chance. We're the only ones who can make honey, pollinate flowers—and well, dress like this. If we're going to survive as a species," he continued, "this is our moment. So, what do you all say? Are we going to be bees?"

"We're bees!" the crowd declared.

"Then follow me!" Barry commanded.

The pollen jock named Buzz stopped him. "Hold

on, Barry," he said. "Here, you've earned this." He held out a pollen collector, along with a jacket and helmet— the official pollen jock uniform.

Barry put on the uniform and grinned widely. "I'm a pollen jock! And it's a perfect fit," he added, examining himself. "Well, except for the sleeves, which are a little long, but I can take them up."

Mr. and Mrs. Benson stood together, proudly watching the scene.

"That's our Barry!" Mrs. Benson beamed.

A moment later the bees returned to work. They landed on the fresh flowers that were strewn along the runway and started collecting pollen. When they were ready, they headed out together.

As the squadron of bees cruised past the control tower, the air traffic controllers saluted them.

Together the bees flew all over the earth, over brown patches of grass, empty window boxes, and fields of dead vegetables and flowers. Bit by bit, they sprinkled pollen over the brown plants. They knew that it wouldn't be long before everything sprung back to life.

In the park, a boy playing with a ball spotted them.

"Look, Mom," he shouted. He pointed toward the sky. "The bees are back! Hurray!"

All over the world humans cheered about the bees' return.

Barry flew over New York City, making sure to pass over Vanessa's apartment building. He dropped down low over her roof terrace, and then he carefully sprinkled pollen over all the flowers in her rooftop garden.

CHAPTER TWENTY

Before long, life in New Hive City was back to normal. Some things about the bees' lives, however, had changed completely.

For one thing, Adam now worked as a tour guide. He told the graduating bees all about making honey at Honex.

"Our annual output is roughly two cups for our own use," he explained, "and in accordance with the new Bee-Human Harmony Act, any surplus honey is given to the humans on an as-needed basis. In return, the humans have made Central Park a non-smoking area."

"Yay!" the graduates cheered.

"We are also now on the Benson flex-time work schedule," Adam explained proudly. "This includes job rotation and a day off each week. Flex time has not only increased our productivity; it has also allowed us to pursue our hobbies and interests."

"Yippee!" cheered the young bees.

Vanessa still played tennis with her friend Ken. But that had changed a bit, too.

One day during a match, Ken hit the ball hard over the net.

Vanessa watched it bounce over the line. "Sorry, Ken, that was out. That's game, set, and match."

"Vanessa!" Ken argued. "That wasn't out. It was on the line!"

They both stepped up to the net.

"Ken. Honestly," Vanessa repeated. "The ball was out. I won."

"It was on the line!" he snapped. "And the line means it's in!"

With a sigh, Vanessa turned toward the umpire. "What do you think?"

Barry sat in a tiny doll's chair wearing a crisp white shirt and a tennis visor. Around his neck was a pair of small binoculars.

"I believe that was out," he said.

Ken's face turned bright red. "You cannot be serious!" he fumed.

"Match to Ms. Bloome," Barry went on. He marked Vanessa's win on the clipboard he used to track their games.

"You are out of your tiny mind, bee!" Ken snapped.

"Ken, it's just a game," Vanessa said gently. "It doesn't matter."

"I hate him!" Ken growled. He threw his racquet down and it bounced up and hit him in his own face. "Ow! Darn it! I can't take this anymore!"

He stomped off the court.

Barry flew over to Vanessa.

"That's a shame," she said. "Tennis was really the best part of our relationship."

Barry nodded. "That Ken is a fierce competitor."

"So what do we do now?" asked Vanessa.

He shrugged.

"I could use a little practice on my serve," she suggested.

"That could be fun," Barry said.

"Really?" she said, surprised. "You don't have to fly out with the pollen jocks or anything?"

"Nope." He shook his head, then smiled. "I have all the time in the world."